'You never ment

'I'm an orphan.' A f
challenge to him.

'So am I,' he said. 'It makes me value family life even more.'

'I could have guessed.'

'I've listened to all your recent radio programmes. Remember a while ago you were talking to someone called Barry?'

In the candlelight his face was a patchwork of planes and shadows. 'You said, "It's a risk you have to take. If you offer something of yourself then you're vulnerable".'

'Yes,' she said carefully. 'But I said a lot more too. You can't take it out of context.'

'That sentence was at the heart of what you said. Why don't you take your own advice?'

'I do!'

'When I asked you why you hadn't got a steady man in your life, you promptly changed the subject. Tell me what you're frightened of. I know there is something.'

Gill Sanderson, aka Roger Sanderson, started as a husband-and-wife team. At first Gill created the storyline, characters and background, asking Roger to help with the actual writing. But her job became more and more time-consuming and he took over all of the work. He loves it!

Roger has written many Medical Romance™ books for Harlequin Mills & Boon®. Ideas come from three of his children—Helen is a midwife, Adam a health visitor, Mark a consultant oncologist. Weekdays are for work; weekends find Roger walking in the Lake District or Wales.

Recent titles by the same author:

MALE MIDWIFE
MARRIAGE AND MATERNITY
THE CONSULTANT'S RECOVERY
A DOCTOR'S HONOUR

HER UNEXPECTED FAMILY

BY
GILL SANDERSON

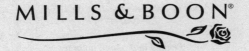

MILLS & BOON®

All the characters in this book have no existence outside the imagination
of the author, and have no relation whatsoever to anyone bearing the
same name or names. They are not even distantly inspired by any
individual known or unknown to the author, and all the incidents are
pure invention.

First published in Great Britain 2002
Harlequin Mills & Boon Limited,
Eton House, 18-24 Paradise Road, Richmond, Surrey TW9 1SR

© Gill Sanderson 2002

ISBN 0 263 83095 0

Set in Times Roman 10½ on 12 pt.
03-1002-47911

Printed and bound in Spain
by Litografia Rosés, S.A., Barcelona

CHAPTER ONE

JUST an ordinary afternoon.

Not that there were any ordinary afternoons in Halstead Hospital Accident and Emergency Department. They were all frantically busy. There had been no chance for Staff Nurse Tessa Calvert to have even a drink since the fifteen minutes she had allowed herself at lunchtime. The triage nurse had kept her busy.

She was working with her friend Jack Harris, the young senior house officer. Together they had dealt with a young woman with a badly scalded arm—the kettle handle had come off. Fortunately only the epithelial layers of skin were affected so she was treated with analgesics, aspiration of the blisters and Flamazine dressing.

Then there had been the boy playing football in the street. He had tripped and fallen, using an outstretched hand to break the fall. So he had broken his wrist and it needed attention.

Eighty-six-year-old Emily Brice had collapsed in the street outside her house and been brought in by a number of concerned friends and relatives. Jack thought she had suffered a TIA—a transient ischaemic attack. After taking a detailed history they had admitted Emily for further investigation. This wasn't made easy by the fact that Emily was demanding to go home, and her relations were demanding an explanation of what was wrong and an instant cure.

'I think I prefer it when patients are brought in on their own,' Jack mumbled.

'They're all worried about her, they love her. You know that's a good thing.'

'I do. But I wish they wouldn't ask questions I can't answer. "Why did it have to happen today?" one woman asked. "It's when she goes to bingo." When I said I just didn't know she obviously thought I was a pretty poor doctor.'

Tessa smiled. 'I'm sure you'll get over it. Now, look, we're not wanted for a while. Let's sneak a cup of coffee.'

It was four o'clock. They had their coffee and then Tessa collected Junior Nurse Sally Kent. She was mentoring the young girl, and took her teaching responsibilities very seriously. She and Sally would work together on techniques of pain relief for a while and then she could get away promptly at five.

Things were going well then at ten to five the curtain was swished aside and Jack said, 'Got an emergency cardiac arrest coming in by ambulance. I could do with a hand.'

Tessa frowned. 'Isn't Fay Roberts available?'

'She appears to be doing something else,' said Jack, looking at her expressionlessly. So Tessa finished with Sally and hurried along with Jack to meet the ambulance. 'Fay Roberts is useless as well as idle,' said Jack when they were alone, 'as you know very well. And nobody does anything about it.'

Tessa did know but she wasn't going to say so. They walked to the glass-covered forecourt where the ambulance would pull in, and Jack went on, 'Anyhow, things might change soon. When this new consultant comes he'll put things in order. There'll be no more putting up with slackers like Fay. I gather he's been here a while, bought himself a house, had no end of meeting with the high-ups. Bit of a whizkid. Not like our Francis Pell.'

Tessa sighed. Francis Pell, their present consultant, was about to retire. Some said that he had retired years ago. 'We'll just have to wait and see,' she said. But secretly she agreed with Jack. The department was getting slack.

The ambulance drew up in front of them and smartly reversed into the bay. As the doors opened Jack scrambled inside, nodding to the green-coated paramedic who was leaning over the still figure. 'What have you got for me?' he asked.

Jack listened to the paramedic's report as Tessa supervised the removal of the patient to the resus room. Other nurses were there, waiting. This was a well-drilled team-based operation in which everyone knew their part.

The man was moved onto his side, gentle oropharangeal suction applied to clear out any saliva and then an airway introduced. Now he could be given oxygen. His clothes were cut away to make venous access easier, and a nurse fixed up a giving set. Cardiac monitoring was arranged, as well as a pulse oximeter and a BM reading. His temperature was checked and an ECG performed, just to check on progress. And slowly, the man seemed to recover. 'I think we'll hand this one on,' Jack said after ten minutes. 'He's more or less out of danger now. Tessa, do you want to phone the cardiac ward?'

'My pleasure,' Tessa said. She checked to see that

all the tests had been recorded properly, ready to be handed over with the patient. 'Anyone found out who he is yet?'

'Working on it,' said another nurse who was looking through a wallet. 'I know where he lives now.'

It was a joint operation they had performed before. It always gave Tessa pleasure to see how smoothly they worked together. But what was the time?

After handover it was six before she got away. Just another ordinary afternoon in Halstead Hospital A and E Department. Tessa walked across to the car park, climbed into her ancient little red car and drove home. She had enjoyed her day, and now she was going to enjoy her evening.

Home was a custom-built flat by the sea. In fact, if you stood on a stool in the bathroom you could actually see the sea—sometimes. After years living in nurses' homes, sharing with friends or renting something that wasn't too bad, she had decided to go for what she really wanted. A flat of her own. After all, she was twenty-eight—time to settle down. It had been a financial struggle, but at least she lived in the reasonably-priced North. She had been to a conference in London a year ago and had told an acquaintance there how much her flat had cost. The girl had laughed bitterly and enviously. 'You wouldn't get a dog kennel for that around here.'

So life should have been looking good for Staff Nurse Tessa Calvert. Why, then, so often recently, had she felt vaguely dissatisfied?

First, a quickly made sandwich. Into the bathroom, a shower and then untie the neat pleat and brush out her shoulder-length dark hair. Then, still in her dressing-gown, she sat at her desk and ran through the evening's script. She had rehearsed it, timed it, and she thought it was pretty good. Her eyes flicked over the files neatly stacked on the top of her bookcase. Twenty-eight files, twenty-eight weekly programmes. She was getting to be an old hand at this.

It was still warm out, with the unusual heat of high summer. She pulled on a sleeveless summer dress in blue. It emphasised her long brown legs and was fairly low cut. If you looked smart then you felt smart. It might be a bit non-nurse-like—but, then, who was going to see her?

A twenty-minute drive and she manoeuvred her way into the tiny car park of Radio Seafront. She nodded to June Ritchie, the always-harassed receptionist. 'Busy night?'

'Aren't they all? I don't know why I work here, I could always go down the mines.'

Tessa smiled to herself. She knew that June loved her job, even though she was run off her feet. But she was a forty-five-year-old divorcee who had seen it all. Never again would she enthuse about anything.

Radio Seafront wasn't a big organisation. There was June's reception room which doubled as a waiting room. To one side was a tiny tearoom, bathroom and storeroom. To the other side was the studio. A red light showed that a show was on air.

Tessa gently opened the studio door and slid inside. Silently she waved to Ray Grantham, the station manager, producer and general dogsbody. Ray waved back, without stopping his reading of a list of local happenings—church fêtes, school concerts, local art displays.

Tessa sat in her chair and pulled on the cans—the large earphones she had to wear when broadcasting.

Her script was open in front of her. Ten minutes to go. She breathed deeply, made herself relax. No longer did she need a glass of water by her in case her voice dried up. Now she was an expert.

Nearly her time. Ray held up five fingers as he introduced her. Then he pointed. She was on air.

'Hi, Nurse Tessa Calvert here, hoping to help you with your health and your personal problems. Remember always, I'm not prescribing, I'm suggesting. There's plenty of professional advice available. If you feel in any doubt about anything, then see your GP. Some interesting letters this week…'

She thought it was going well. When she looked at Ray he nodded and smiled. She kept her eye on the clock. If she found she was seriously overrunning she could cut out a little. Broadcasting live was sometimes a bit terrifying! But all was going well.

'I know you've got your pride, Ken, but there are limits. It's just not on for your girlfriend to expect you to pay for everything, especially as you're both students. So try to talk to her again. And if she won't see reason, ask yourself if she's the kind of girl you really want to go out with.

'That's all for this evening. You know the station address. Any queries you think I can help with—remember, you can always ''Ask a Nurse''.'

Ray nodded and as she took off her cans, bent to give the station address again. Ben Yardley, the DJ who would play requests for the next three hours, came and sat next to her, his case of discs ready. Tessa softly walked out of the studio, followed by Ray. 'Another great programme,' said Ray. 'Let's go and celebrate.'

Opposite Radio Seafront was the Black Lion. At

lunchtime it was heaving with local businessmen grabbing a drink and a sandwich. But in the evenings it was always quiet. The sun was still strong as they crossed the street, but the Black Lion had its shades down and inside it was dim, almost intimate.

Ray led her to one of the banquettes and said, 'Special night tonight. Let me pick the drinks. We've done a lot of planning here, haven't we? Now I've got something a bit special for you to think about.' And he went to the bar.

Tessa leaned back against the red plush cushions and consciously relaxed. She was quite used to broadcasting now, but she still felt tired after each show. Probably the consequence of adrenaline.

Vaguely she wondered what Ray had to say that was special. Nothing personal, of course. They were very close friends, but that was all. Ray was twenty years older than her, happily married with two children. Just the kind of man friend she wanted. Anyway, she didn't go out with men she worked with. In fact, she seldom went out with any man. Passion had got her nowhere.

Ray seemed to be quite a while at the bar—she could hear him joking with the barmaid. Once again she thought how lucky she had been to meet him, how well their ideas worked together.

She had written to him with an idea for a programme, which she was willing to do for nothing. It had been a mad idea but her life had seemed a bit, well, flat. He had written back to her and invited her for a drink here in the Black Lion—in fact, in this, their favourite banquette. They had talked, planned, looked at scripts, and now *Ask A Nurse* went out on Radio Seafront every Friday night at half past eight.

It was only a small, local radio station, but Tessa liked to think that she did some good. Listeners were invited to write to her with their personal or medical problems. Every letter got a written reply—and four or five she selected each week to read out and comment on. She was a qualified nurse and had taken a diploma in counselling, but thought that the best qualification for her job was a robust common sense. And the number of letters was growing...

Ray came back, a beaming smile on his face. 'Champagne,' he said, placing two crystal flutes on the table. 'The only drink to celebrate. Here's to us, Tessa.'

She looked at him, perplexed, as he sat opposite her. Usually she had red wine, Ray a pint of beer. 'What are we celebrating, Ray? Why to us?'

Ray didn't answer at first. He drank his champagne, obviously enjoying his moment of suspense. 'Ray! I'm getting all curious here. What are we celebrating?'

'We're celebrating the beginning of our future. Tessa, I'm leaving Radio Seafront. I've been offered a job on a national radio station, doing much what I'm doing now. I'm to develop new programmes— and the one I want to start with is the one I enjoy doing now. I want to take *Ask A Nurse* onto national radio.'

She looked at him, speechless. Then she groped for her champagne.

'Ray, this is just a sideline for me. I'm a nurse, I'm good at it, I like it. I couldn't go on national radio I'd...I'd...'

'You may be a good nurse but you're a born broadcaster. Your voice is great! There's that touch of a northern accent, and it's a warm voice, a friendly one. You've seen the letters when people say how much they like listening to you.'

'But what would we…surely *Ask A Nurse* wouldn't work in its present format?'

'I know that. We'd have to broaden the appeal— have you interview guests, conduct discussions. There's a lot to learn, you'd have to be interviewed first and then go on a training programme. And the money would be more than you're getting now.'

'Like I said, I'm a nurse, Ray. Whatever I do, I won't give that up. It's what keeps me…what I am.'

Ray waved a hand carelessly. 'We'll be working from Manchester, we can sort something out. All I want you to do now is think about it. You know, we've spent hours here, talking about new formats for the show.'

'Yes, we have,' she agreed. Tessa hadn't realised just how seriously Ray had been taking her ideas.

'Just sit there and think about it,' Ray said again. 'There's no hurry. Well, not much.'

She was silent a moment, looking round the interior of the pub. Here she'd spent many quiet happy hours with Ray. He had been so good for her self-confidence. Now she was feeling lost again.

The door banged open and she looked up. Someone must have pushed it with unnecessary force. A dark figure was silhouetted against the sunlight outside. There was something about the hunch of the shoulders, the angle of the neck. She had trained herself to recognise body language—in an A and E department this was often very necessary. This man was upset— no, he was angry.

Behind him the door closed and the man went over

to the bar, quietly ordered a drink and whispered to the barmaid. Tessa was curious. She lifted her glass and peered over its rim, studying this new arrival.

After a moment's conversation the man turned and surveyed the room. He stepped forward and paused, his face illuminated by the nearest wall light. He stared at her directly and, she couldn't help it, she stared back.

He was an attractive man. A very, *very* attractive man.

Tessa had heard it could happen like this. It was strange. A glance exchanged with a complete stranger, a moment's magic communion that suggested an infinity of possibilities. She felt it, she knew he had, too. Tessa bit back a gasp. Just what had she seen in this man's eyes?

Then the moment passed, the man looked away. And she remembered that she was twenty-eight years old, a sensible, serious professional. She didn't believe in instant romantic attachments—she didn't want a romantic attachment of any kind. She was tired, that was all. But for a moment... She turned back to Ray.

'This could be my big chance,' Ray went on, 'and I think that with you I—'

'Miss Calvert and Mr Grantham? Mind if I join you?'

The voice was curt. It was obvious that the man didn't care whether they minded or not. He slammed his glass on the table and before they could object had pulled up a chair and sat at the end of their banquette.

Tessa felt the first prickle of apprehension. He knew her name. Had the man misunderstood her interest? He had set his chair so they couldn't get out without disturbing him. And there was an impression of power and strength as he leaned forward and stared at both of them.

Then she noticed that the open-necked shirt was an expensive one, made of fine white linen. The hands that rested on the table were broad but the fingernails were clean and well cut. This man took pains with his appearance.

His face was now alarming. He might have been quite good-looking if he smiled and she liked his longish dark hair. But a generous mouth was spoiled by tight-pressed lips and the large grey eyes were now smouldering with barely veiled fury.

There were deep lines round eyes and mouth which she recognised as lines of fatigue. This man was obviously very tired. And his stillness only emphasised the fury that was within him.

'We'd like to help you,' Ray tried gently, 'but this is a private conversation. If you'd like to ask Reception at the station I'm sure they could…'

The man ignored Ray, dismissed him without speaking. Ray's voice tailed away. The man looked only at Tessa now, glanced at her rather exposed front. It took all the strength she had to keep her hands by her side, not to reach and pull up the front of her dress. She wouldn't do it!

The stranger spoke. 'Just what I expected. I might have known you'd be a young attractive thing.'

'I don't think there's any need to…' Ray tried to interrupt, but the man overrode him, his eyes fixed on Tessa. 'I'm here to get an explanation from you about the rubbish you've been broadcasting. I want to know if you realise the harm you're doing.'

Tessa knew that the advice she gave didn't suit everyone. She'd had the occasional letter saying so. But so far no one had actually called on her. She didn't like it, it was a bit frightening.

Ray tried again, and this time the man let him finish. 'If you have any complaints they should be addressed to me. I see all of Miss Calvert's scripts, vet them if you like.'

The man smiled, but it wasn't a happy smile. 'Then you'd better listen, too. I may well be suing the station as well as this young lady who calls herself a relationship expert.'

'Suing?' Ray said, obviously taken aback. 'That's a bit excessive, isn't it?'

'I don't think so. You're supposed to be offering a public service. Every public service may be sued if it gets things seriously wrong. I certainly know that.'

Tessa saw that Ray didn't like this threat. Certainly she was sure the man had no cause for complaint. But a determined man, even if he were wrong, could do a considerable amount of damage.

At first she had been rather frightened, nervous of this tall, angry stranger. But now she was getting angry. She wanted to shout at the man, to ask him who he thought he was, what did he mean making these stupid comments? No. What was needed was anger management. She had been trained in how to defuse situations, how to calm people without giving them the satisfaction of having a fight. There had to be some way of discussing this man's problems calmly.

The trouble was, he was obviously intelligent. She didn't know how she knew this, whether it was the voice or the dark light in his eye. But she was willing to bet that this man was no fool. He wasn't some kind

of fanatic and somehow that made him more dangerous.

'I'm sure we can talk about your problem calmly,'
she said, 'and go about things in a rational and reasonable manner.'

She was pleased with her little speech, delivered in
just the right cold tones. But the man wasn't impressed.

'You can be calm and rational and reasonable. But
I'm too tired to be all those things. I'm furious. I've
had two hard days. And in between I was up all night
chasing down to London to pick up my daughter who
ran away from home because of your advice. The
advice of a halfwit!'

Tessa had had enough. Sweetly, she said, 'I'm
sorry about your daughter. But do you find abuse
more productive than explaining what's wrong? Quite
frankly, I think that's the action of a halfwit.'

Beside her, she felt Ray flinch. The man's face
darkened with anger. He was shocked to be addressed
in this way. But she held her gaze, her blue eyes
trying to outstare his grey ones. And after a while he
looked away.

From his pocket he took a letter and put it on the
table. 'All right, we will be calm,' he said softly.
'This letter was sent from you to my daughter. Would
you like to check?'

Her fingers trembling slightly, she opened the letter. 'Yes, my letter, my signature.'

'And what made things worse, you repeated this
advice on your radio programme. You have a very
persuasive voice, Miss Calvert.'

Tessa was reading through her letter. She remembered the case quite well. A girl had written in to say

that she had been brought up by her father. He'd been good while she was a child, but now he thought he was still entitled to dominate her. She was looking forward to being eighteen when she'd technically be an adult but her father made her work non-stop and wouldn't let her have any social life. She earned some money but he wouldn't let her spend it. She had fallen for a young man a few years older than her but her father wouldn't let her see him. Now they had moved well away from her boyfriend. What should she do?

Tessa had advised the girl that probably her father still loved her. They should try to discuss things. But she was an individual with a right to her own feelings. She should show her father this. She should try to talk him round. And if this didn't work she should go her own way, show him she was an individual.

'I can't really see what you're objecting to,' she said to the man, 'I think the advice I gave is quite correct. I stand by every word of it. At this age a girl is entitled to her own life.'

'Quite so.' The voice was even softer now, and Tessa found herself wishing that he would get angry again. She could cope with that. But she had an uneasy feeling that she had led herself into a trap. How?

'My daughter is fortunate, she has a skill that has enabled her to earn, well, reasonable sums of money. She is tall, has matured early, and like many young women she thinks she knows her own mind.'

'Perhaps she does know her own mind,' Tessa put in.

'Perhaps. I don't think so. She is a very gifted musician and has been since she was eight. I want her to train so that she can have a musical career. The money she earns now is irrelevant.'

'But you can't live an eighteen-year-old's life for her!'

'Of course I can't. I hope I wouldn't want to. But what about a fourteen-year-old? What if she wants to go out with a twenty-one-year-old of very doubtful reputation?'

'Fourteen-year-old!' Tessa gazed at him in horror. 'My advice was for an eighteen-year-old! Very different from what I'd say to someone aged fourteen!'

The man picked up the letter, glanced at it. 'You don't say that. I would have thought it important.'

'But…she said she was looking forward to being eighteen! I thought that she was seventeen. She hid things from me!'

'I gather you're a nurse, Miss Calvert, and you work in an A and E department. Can't you tell when patients are lying to you? Don't you know how to get at the truth?'

While Tessa thought about this the man finished his drink. An orange juice, she noted, not what she would have expected. He stood, empty glass in hand, and said, 'I'm going to get myself another drink, I need one. Don't think of going away, though. We've got more talking to do.' Then he paused, irresolute. She knew what was going through his mind. It wasn't in his nature to get himself a drink and not those he was sitting with. She felt pleased at his predicament. He said, 'Since we're sitting together, could I—?'

'Not for either of us thank you,' Tessa said.

He glared at her, obviously not used to being interrupted, but then left without a further word.

She thought about what he had just said. Staff in A and E were often lied to. There were wives coming in with black eyes, facial injuries, who had 'had a

fall'. There were young lads who had over-
dosed—'Someone must have put it in my drink.'
There were the drivers who were over the limit—'I've
been taking antibiotics, they must have affected me.'
She recognised these stories for the lies they were.
Why hadn't she spotted that this letter was, well, at
least ambiguous?

The man returned. 'I've reread my letter,' Tessa
said, 'and I think I stand by everything I say. It was
just taken at the wrong time.'

'It's not our fault if the girl lied,' Ray chipped in.
Tessa sighed to herself. That had not been the right
thing to say—or the right time to say it.

'Not your fault? Passing the buck as usual?'

'We're sorry that you've been put to this trouble,'
Tessa apologised hurriedly. 'What would you like us
to do? Naturally we're very eager to put things right.'

'Naturally,' the man said. 'In fact, there is something you can do. You can put right the damage you
have done and come to talk to my daughter.'

'Perhaps Miss Calvert has other things she needs
to do,' Ray said sharply. 'We don't operate a home
visit service.'

'Last night I had other things I needed to do.
Instead of doing them, I had to drive to London, find
my daughter and drive back.'

'No way will Miss Calvert go to the home of a
man she doesn't know—whether she wants to or not!'

The man smiled. 'If Miss Calvert doesn't know me
yet, she soon will.' He dropped a card onto the table.
'My name is James Armstrong. I'm the new consultant in Halstead Hospital A and E Department. Miss
Calvert, I'm your new boss.'

Tessa thought that there didn't seem to be much anyone could say to that.

After a while James Armstrong said, 'I know you finish at five tomorrow and then you've got three days off. I suggest you get to my house at about seven. You can talk to my daughter, try to undo the harm you have done.'

'What if she still doesn't want to?' Ray asked desperately.

'I'm sure she does. For one thing there's her professional pride. My daughter thinks she makes sense, Miss Calvert will want to put her right. She talked her into this rebellion, she can talk her out of it again.'

'Or you'll phone your solicitor?'

'That's right, Miss Calvert. And it wouldn't be good for your career—or the radio station—to be involved in this kind of situation. Goodnight.'

Tessa watched him walk out of the door, momentarily outlined again against the sunlight. It was a confident walk, the walk of a man who was sure he had won. And, of course, he *had* won.

'He has no real case, you know,' Ray said after a pause. 'We'll stand by you. What do you want to do?'

Tessa knew that there was only one course of action. 'If he does cause trouble there goes your chance at a new job and there goes my hopes of working with you. I'll go and see this daughter. For two reasons. First, I want to undo any harm I might have done. Second, any child of that man needs all the help she can get.'

'Maybe you're right. I'm going to get us both another drink. I think we need one.'

Tessa's heart was beating far faster than it should have. I've just had an argument, she told herself. It was unpleasant, I'm stressed, of course my heart is beating faster. On a personal level that man means nothing to me.

But she remembered that moment when her eyes had met his, and she wondered if this were true.

James Armstrong strode out of the Black Lion and walked quickly to his car. He drove out of the town centre, then took a side road that led to the coast, where there was a car park. He locked his car then walked along the beachside path until he came to a bench. As good a place as any to sit and think.

Seagulls were screaming overhead, he could hear the distant thump of a tanker's engines and see the ship pushing out to sea about a mile away. It should have been peaceful there in the late sunshine. But he wasn't at peace with himself.

He'd done it again. He'd lost his temper, tried to bully people when there had been no need. That nurse's rebuke had probably been deserved. He *had* acted like a halfwit. The fact that he was concerned about his daughter was no excuse.

The nurse—Tessa Calvert? He remembered the first glimpse he'd had of her when he'd caught her looking at him. For a second his anger had been forgotten, all he'd been able to think of had been how gorgeous she was. And something had passed between them, a recognition of… He shook his head angrily. He was being ridiculous!

But she was gorgeous. Her hair was thick and dark, falling to her shoulders, and when she turned her head quickly she had to brush it from her eyes. Her eyes were blue, candid but capable of blazing with anger.

He wondered if she knew how attractive she was when she was angry.

In some ways it was a pity her programme only went out on radio, she would have been an instant success on television. Her face was not merely beautiful, it was alive. When she smiled or frowned or looked thoughtful, he knew at once what she was feeling.

If she hadn't misled his daughter, if he didn't have to work with her, if they hadn't started in such a bad way, perhaps they could have... No. He had a new job in a slack department and a fourteen-year-old daughter to cope with. He didn't have time for passionate attachments. Look where it had got him last time.

But Tessa *was* gorgeous.

CHAPTER TWO

'WE USE the Glasgow coma scale for initial neuro-
logical observations,' Tessa said to the junior nurse.
'How do you calculate it?'

'We give a score for each of eye-opening, verbal
response and motor response,' Sally replied. 'There's
a total maximum score of fifteen and…'

Later on Saturdays was when A and E would be
really busy. They had a very quiet morning so Tessa
was running through one or two points with Sally.
She enjoyed this teaching, not least because it kept
things fresh in her mind. She thought an odd half-
hour practical lesson was more useful than a day's
note-taking in a classroom.

'Let's go mad, Tessa,' Jack said to her at half past
twelve. 'Let's do something really reckless. How
about taking the full lunch-break we're entitled to and
going to the canteen? Have egg and chips on me.'

'I like a man who can show a girl a good time.'
Tessa smiled. 'You're on. And if we don't get bleeped
before we've finished that, I'll treat you to syrup
sponge and custard.'

'A positive feast! Let's go, Nurse Calvert.'

She liked the young SHO. He was keen, hard-
working, vastly enthusiastic. And he'd shown a skill
with patients that was greater than his youthful appearance would have suggested. He understood people. Tessa thought she'd ask him about the chance

she had of working for national radio. His opinion
would be worth having.

She didn't even dream of telling him about her en-
counter with James Armstrong. That was private—
and embarrassing. And somehow she knew that her
new boss would never mention what had happened in
the Black Lion to anyone in the department. Not if
she didn't. This was business purely between the two
of them.

The egg and chips were good. 'I've had a job offer,' she said as they tucked in. 'I'd like to know what
you think, Jack.'

He was silent as she outlined what Ray had suggested to her. Then he said, 'I think it's a great chance
for you, Tessa. It's something you'd be good at.
But…' He frowned and scratched his head. 'Basically
you're a nurse. It's what you're best at. If you did
nothing but radio programmes, I think in a while you
might lose that touch you've got. You're good on the
radio because you're good with people. People listen
to you because they feel you know what you're talking about. And that comes from nursing.'

It was a long speech for Jack. She thought about
what he had said and decided he made sense—it was
what she had thought herself. She would only do the
programmes if she could be a nurse as well.

'I think you're probably right, Jack,' she agreed.

'Good. And that brings me to the real purpose of
this lunchtime treat.'

Quietly, Tessa sighed. She suspected she knew
what was coming, it had been coming for a while.
She and Jack were friends, but there had been hints,
indications that he wanted more. His arm round her
shoulder for longer than necessary. His hand resting

on hers when she gave him his mug of coffee. It was a pity it had to come to this.

Jack didn't notice her reserve. 'Next Saturday there's a party at the hospital social club. Sister Jepson has been married for thirty years and everyone's going to help her celebrate. How would you like to come as my partner?'

She didn't want to be hurtful but she had to make her position clear. 'I'd love to come with you, Jack. But there's one thing you've got to know, and with me it's an iron rule. I never have a relationship with anyone I work with.'

'Relationship. You mean like—?'

'I want to be friends. But there can never be anything…more between us.' Perhaps it was better to be blunt.

'Why not? Most married people I know met each other at work. And they're happy.' He wasn't being awkward, he really wanted to know.

'I know. It's just that I don't think that work and romance mix. Now, I'd love to go with you, Jack, but only as a friend. Perhaps if we could go in a group?'

He shook his head sadly. 'That's fine if that's what you want. But I warn you, I'm going to write to this woman I heard on the radio and ask her for advice. She was good last night. I particularly liked her advice that if the woman doesn't pay half then get rid of her.'

'But they're both students! I'm a low paid nurse and you're a highly paid doctor! Still, I promise to buy you a pint.'

Then they both laughed and she felt happy. Jack had taken her rebuff well. They would stay friends.

But as they walked back to the A and E department

she thought of what he had said. Most of the people she knew had met their partner at work. Where might she meet someone? She had very little social life outside work. But, then, after all that had happened in her life, did she want a partner?

There was work as soon as they arrived back. A seventeen-year-old lad was brought in, suffering from headache, tremors and tachycardia. He knew himself what was wrong. 'I'm a diabetic,' he managed to mumble. Tessa took a quick history and knew instantly what was wrong. 'He's hypoglycaemic,' she muttered to Jack. 'I've tried, but I can't get him to drink anything.' Sometimes a drink loaded with sugar could have a remarkable effect.

Jack glanced at her notes. He knew that Tessa knew as much about this as he did. 'The usual,' he said. 'Put in a cannula and give him fifty mil of dextrose.'

'May I get Sally to do it? We can watch her.'

'Good idea.'

They watched and saw the usual dramatic recovery. But the lad would be monitored and not sent home until the staff were certain that his system was functioning properly again.

'I've got a meeting later on with the new chief,' Jack murmured as they watched. 'He says he wants to have a word with all the doctors privately first, then try to organise a meeting for as many people as he can get together.'

Tessa nodded. Although it was the A and E consultant's department, technically he wasn't in charge of the nursing staff. 'Have you heard anything about him?' she asked, striving to sound casual. 'What's the gossip?'

She knew how small the world of medicine could

be. Even though James Armstrong had come two hundred miles north from London, there would be someone in the hospital who knew of him or had worked with him.

'He's supposed to be a tough man with a temper. He works like mad and he expects everyone else to do the same. Apparently he turned round a department in a South London hospital—changed it from a slapdash place to one that was super-efficient. But he's fair. Work with him and he'll work with you.'

Jack stepped forward and watched as Sally carefully extracted the cannula. Then he came back and said, 'I'm looking forward to him being here. There's a lot of slack in the department.'

'Can't wait to meet him,' said Tessa.

She considered what Jack had said. Well, she would see. She had thought a lot about the letter she had sent to the man's daughter, and had decided it had been largely right. It wasn't her fault if the girl had concealed her age. And if James Armstrong wanted a fight, he could have one.

In an hour she was going to meet James Armstrong and his daughter and she couldn't make up her mind what to wear. Clothes were important. If you looked good, you felt good. And clothes made an instant impression. She wanted her dress to say something to Armstrong—though she wasn't sure what.

If it was too casual it would upset the father, if it was too formal it might frighten the daughter. She had to get it just right. Eventually she decided on a dark grey dress, suitably long and rather severe. No one could object to her in this. She would feel no urge to pull at the front of it.

Yesterday's good weather had disappeared. There was a cold wind from the estuary and it was raining a little. She put on a light mac and picked up her umbrella. Then she set off in plenty of time. She intended to arrive, cool and collected, at exactly seven.

His house wasn't too far from her flat, situated in a pleasant, leafy suburb further up the coast, handy for the city by railway. She rather liked the house. It was largish, detached, quite old. There was a wide drive lined by mature trees.

On the wall was an estate agent's board with a 'sold' sign on it. It struck her that he must have moved fast to get a house so quickly. Was moving fast a part of his character? It struck her it might well be. In A and E it was often necessary to make quick decisions. So long as they were the right ones.

She parked her car and walked to the porch. There she waited a minute, feeling just a touch nervous. From inside the house she could hear piano music, a brilliant piece, extremely difficult to play. Then it stopped and a passage was repeated, slightly more slowly. She realised that it wasn't recorded music— someone in the house was actually playing.

She took her finger from the doorbell, not wanting to disturb the player inside. For a moment she was rapt—and then the door was jerked open.

It was James Armstrong, scowling. His sheer physical presence gave her a shock, she had forgotten the impression of masculinity he gave out. He was an imposing figure, now dressed in a dark T-shirt and cream chinos.

'Too frightened to knock?' he asked. 'You could have waited there all night but I saw your car in the drive.'

'I wasn't frightened at all, Mr Armstrong,' she said, lying. 'I was waiting for the music to finish, I was enjoying it. A Chopin mazurka, isn't it?'

He opened the door further, gesturing for her to come in. 'It is a Chopin mazurka. If I said I was surprised at your knowing that, would you be offended?'

'Yes,' she said, meeting his gaze.

He said nothing to this, but helped her off with her coat and hung it in a little cloakroom, placing her umbrella in a stand. She hadn't expected this courtesy and it threw her a bit.

'I started to learn to play the piano as a child,' Tessa said, 'I enjoyed it but then…'

'So many start and so many give up.'

Not for the reasons I did, Tessa thought, but said nothing. A loud and brilliant passage echoed down the corridor and she remembered why she was here. 'Is that your daughter playing the piano? She's so good!'

'She is indeed. Yes, it is my daughter, the same one you advised to go and follow her love. Her would-be boyfriend, incidentally, thinks that music doesn't exist if it isn't electronically enhanced. Shall we go to my study?'

It was much quieter when they entered the study and he had shut the door. She liked the room. It was large, panelled in a dark red wood. There was a rich Persian carpet on the floor, bookcases along three walls with medical prints ranged along the top of them. Obviously it was a workroom. To the side of the oak desk was a computer and there were boxes of magazines, and files piled in one corner. There was also a coffee-table between two leather easy chairs. You could work or relax in this room.

He waved her to a seat facing his desk and sat opposite her. 'I'll take you to see Lucy in a moment. But first of all let's get things straight. You need to know the facts as I see them.'

'I might have my own view of the same facts.'

He looked surprised at this interruption. 'Possibly. You'll have the chance to correct me if I am wrong.'

Often a doctor in an A and E department had to brief his staff. It was necessary to put all the relevant facts before people, if possible in order of importance, and then make sure that they knew precisely what their duties were. Some doctors were better at it than others. Their retiring consultant, Francis Pell, was terrible. He would ramble, contradict himself, take far too long and then leave his staff with no clear idea of what they were to do. By comparison James Armstrong was a miracle of lucidity.

'My daughter is fourteen and a very competent musician. She will probably make it her career—if she works hard enough. I took up the post of consultant in A and E here about a month ago. Lucy had to leave her school and go to a new one here, leave her friends and come with me. Naturally it distressed her, but I thought she was settling down. Then she wrote to you, listened to your advice and ran away to London. I knew where she would be. It wasn't a serious running away, she was just—as you recommended—''showing me she was an individual''. And there was no problem getting her back. I drove down there, I knew she'd be staying with a girl friend, and I brought her straight back.'

'So what do you think I should do?'

He looked at her in some surprise. 'I should have thought that was obvious. Tell her that your advice was rubbish.'

He sighed and rubbed his face, and for a moment Tessa felt sorry for him. No matter how stubborn he was being, it was obvious he only wanted what he thought was best for his daughter.

'In a fortnight I have to go to France for three days to a conference. Lucy was supposed to stay with her friend's family, but now she has some mad idea of staying in London and going to a party. I just won't have that and I can't risk leaving her here now. So I have to take her to a hotel in France where she'll be bored silly and I won't be able to concentrate on my work. All because of your so-called advice.'

Tessa felt it was time she defended herself. This man was getting away with too much. 'Mr Armstrong, it was perfectly good advice—but for an eighteen-year-old, not a fourteen-year-old. If she wants to talk to me I'll definitely tell her off for trying to deceive me.'

James Armstrong looked at her approvingly, possibly for the first time. 'Good! And what you'll tell her is—'

'What I'll tell her is for me to decide. You're a doctor, you do what you think is best for your patients. I'm a counsellor, I do the same.' She met his scowl with a serene but firm smile.

It was ages before he spoke. 'Very well. It looks like I have no choice. But I warn you, counsellor. If you make a decision, you stand by the consequences. This afternoon I heard about how you've been offered a job on radio. It would be a pity if I had to stop that.'

'You wouldn't! You couldn't!'

'Wouldn't? Couldn't? Not two words I like to hear, Nurse Calvert.'

She wondered how he knew about the job offer, and guessed that Jack had mentioned it. He wouldn't have done it deliberately, though. Had their boss brought her into the conversation, asked about her? She wouldn't put it past him. Still, that was for the future.

'Tell me more about Lucy, tell me about the family. I take it there's no mother?'

'No.' That answer was curt, definitive. There was to be no discussion. 'Look, is all this necessary? All you have to do is—'

'Of course it's necessary! A situation like this doesn't exist in a vacuum, the entire family is involved.'

'I hope you don't think that you're going to counsel me! I'm beginning to think that I should have—'

'Who's this, then?' The voice was defiant.

Tessa looked up, not having heard the study door open.

'Lucy, this is Nurse Tessa Calvert, the lady on the radio who advised you.' Armstrong's tone was flat.

Tessa stood, held out her hand. 'Hello, Lucy.'

Lucy was a tall, good-looking girl, with her father's dark hair and generous mouth. She also had her father's scowling expression. Was it a family trait? After a hesitation that was just long enough to be very rude, she accepted Tessa's hand, squeezed it briefly and dropped it.

Father and daughter stared at each other. Tessa thought she could detect a bond between them—of love and respect. But there was also defiance on the daughter's part and exasperation on the father's.

Lucy turned back to Tessa. 'So he's got you in his side now?'

Just like her father. Come out fighting. The best thing to do was remain calm.

'No, I don't take sides. And if I was anyone's side, it would be yours.'

She had to move fast before she lost all the initiative. Turning to Armstrong, she said, 'I'd like to talk to Lucy in private. If I need to talk to the pair of you together, I'll ask.'

She could tell he didn't like that, but to her surprise he didn't argue. 'All right, I'll risk it. You can go to Lucy's room. I've been asking about you, you've got a very good reputation in the A and E department.' To keep her in place, he added, 'Slightly to my surprise. You'll report back to me afterwards?'

'No. Lucy and I might come to talk to you. But anything she wants to say to me in confidence, she can.'

'Listen, Dad—' Lucy started, and Tessa touched her arm.

'Let's go,' she said. 'Where's this room of yours?' And Lucy allowed herself to be led out of the study.

Lucy's room was as pleasant as the study. In the centre of the room was a grand piano. There was also an expensive hi-fi system and a display of certificates and medals for music. But there were also teenager magazines scattered round and a collection of dolls on a shelf. It was a lived-in room.

Often in A and E there wasn't time to take a really detailed history. But now Tessa had time. She sat in the easy chair Lucy kicked her way and talked generally about anything that came into her head. This settling of a patient was what she was good at.

Slowly, Lucy started to talk back. Instead of replying in monosyllables, she gave thought-out answers. Instead of wandering round the room, she pulled up a stool and sat opposite Tessa. And Tessa started to like the girl.

Lucy was awkward. She was lonely, she was troubled but she was likeable. Worst of all, she was growing up, and it seemed her father wasn't coping with it very well. After a while Tessa introduced the subject—why had Lucy run away?

'I don't suppose you'd believe me if I said I was in love,' Lucy said, still sounding sullen.

'I'd believe you if you said you thought you were in love.'

'What's the difference? Anyway, what do you know about being in love?'

Tessa hesitated, but she liked Lucy and wanted to help her. And she thought she could trust her.

'I know all about being in love,' she said. 'It's when you can't think of anything but him. If you're working, you look forward to that five minutes you can phone him at night. When he walks towards you, your heart bumps and you feel as if you're floating. You'll do anything to make him happy, and all he has to do to make you happy is to hold your hand or kiss you or hug you. You ignore all your old friends and family, this man is the centre of your life. Nothing else matters.'

Lucy had remained silent during this speech. Now she said, 'You've been there, you've felt it, you're just like me! You do know what it's like!'

'Yes,' said Tessa, after a pause. 'And when I told him I was pregnant he wanted nothing to do with me and threw me out of our flat.'

There was silence for a minute. Then Lucy said, 'Is that a true story or did you make it up?'

'It's a true story. Every last miserable fact in it.'

'Was it meant to shock me? Because it didn't. Things are different between Dan and me.'

'Where have I heard that before? Things are always different in your own case. Are you sure my story didn't shock you?'

Lucy didn't answer. Instead, she leapt to her feet and said, 'That's enough talking for now. Would you like me to play for you?'

'I'd like that very much,' Tessa said sincerely. 'I really would.'

So for ten minutes Lucy played Chopin and Tessa sat and listened. Lucy was good. She had more than mere technical skill, there was feeling in her music. Tessa wondered if she was listening to someone who in time might be great.

Suddenly Lucy stopped. 'That's enough music,' she said. 'Let's talk some more.'

'All right.' Tessa tried to keep her pleasure hidden. If Lucy wanted to talk then half her problems were over. Now was the time to press. 'You're not really wanting to see more of this Dan, are you? Maybe you're just trying to teach your dad a lesson.'

'That's rubbish! Just because he's older than me and people think he's...' Lucy's voice trailed away. More quietly she said, 'I think I recognised what you were talking about when you were telling me what love was like.'

'I'm sure you did. Are you lonely up here, Lucy?'

Lucy shrugged. 'I'm never lonely when I've got my music. I quite like the new school I go to and Dad's found me a super music teacher. But I haven't got any new friends yet. And Dad's so busy—he just doesn't understand me. I feel a bit…well, lost.'

'So it's not really about Dan, is it? My letter was just an excuse—you wanted to teach your dad a lesson. Irritate him, make him notice you more.'

'He overreacted didn't he?' Lucy was obviously half-pleased at the thought.

Tessa thought that he *had* overreacted but no way was she going to say so. 'It's possible. But only because he loves you. Now, do you want to ask me for the advice I'd give to a fourteen-year-old in your situation?'

'Go on,' said Lucy.

'I don't need to, you know already what I'm going to say. You've heard it a dozen times.'

'And how. This is difficult time…blah, blah, blah…hormones and adolescence…blah, blah, blah…got to keep loving and trusting…blah, blah, blah. My advice is…'

After a pause Tessa clapped. 'Perfect.' She smiled. 'You know the script better than I do. Now, as you know the answer already, why bother asking me the question?'

Lucy looked at her quizzically. 'You're quite hard, aren't you?'

'Try tough, not hard. In A and E—where both your dad and I work—you've got to be that way. Now, without getting angry, why don't you go and negotiate with him? Calmly and quietly, no confrontation or shouting. Tell him you're sorry but explain why you did it. Say you need a little more space for yourself as you're getting to be a young woman.'

'You think he'll buy that? My dad who knows everything?'

'He might,' said Tessa after some consideration. 'You can at least try him. What's the minimum you'd settle for? He says you want to go to some kind of party in London. Just how important is it to you?'

When Lucy didn't have her sullen expression on she was a very attractive girl. Tessa watched her as she thought. 'How about if I say I'll give up Dan and going to the party? But I get to go to stay with my friends in London and I'm let out at night a bit more here?'

'Sounds a basis for discussion. Try him.' Tessa frowned. 'You're willing to give up Dan? Five minutes ago you were madly in love with him.'

'That's teenagers for you,' said Lucy with a giggle. 'You just can't trust them. Shall I go and see my dad now?' Then her face fell. 'Did he tell you about this trip to France?'

'He mentioned it. If you're interested, he feels guilty about having to take you and then abandon you. Why not tell him you'll put up with it somehow?'

'Guess you're right. OK, talk over, I'm off to be reasonable.'

Tessa stayed in Lucy's room, her heart thumping. She wondered if she'd said and done the right things. Of course, this hadn't been true counselling. It had been simple common sense. She hoped that the girl's father would see it that way. Whatever was being said, it was taking a long time. It was quite twenty minutes since Lucy had left the room.

'Miss Calvert. Sorry to leave you on your own so long.'

Tessa looked up, blinked. It was James Armstrong himself who had returned to the room, Lucy just be-

hind him. She stood. 'All going well?' she asked
hopefully.

'Remarkably well. Could I invite you to have a
glass of wine with me in my study?'

This was a totally different James Armstrong to the
one she'd met previously. 'I'd love a glass of wine,'
she said. 'See you in a while Lucy.'

As she walked down the passage she heard behind
her the triumphant sounds of one of Chopin's polo-
naises. It seemed that Lucy was pleased with life, too.

This time Tessa didn't sit facing him at his desk.
Instead, she was directed to one of the easy chairs by
the coffee-table. He asked her if a dry Saumur would
do. She said yes, sipped it and decided that it would
do very well indeed. This bottle hadn't come from the
supermarket.

He sat opposite her and for the first time seemed a
little ill at ease. 'In half an hour you seem to have
got further with my daughter than I have in six
months,' he said. 'I now know where I went wrong
and so does Lucy. We've worked out some kind of a
living plan and I hope we'll both be able to stick to
it. I want you to know that I'm truly grateful.'

'So no threat to sue?'

He looked abashed. 'No threat to sue. It was a complete error on my part. I judged you entirely wrongly
and I'm very sorry.'

It was a handsome apology, unasked-for, and she
wondered how much it had cost him to make it. She
thought that this showed he was a man of principle
who would have to do what he thought right, no matter how painful. Such people could be dangerous.

'I can only say that she is my daughter and I...
You have no children, do you?'

'No, but I was a child myself. You don't need to have children to know about families.'

He looked at her shrewdly. 'That was said with more than a little feeling. You've had problems of your own?'

She had to cover up. 'No more than anyone else. I know families and I have had counselling training.'

'Well, I have to thank you.'

'About Lucy's mother. Could I ask…?'

It was the completely wrong question. His face darkened and she saw the scowling man of old again. 'No, you could not,' he snapped. 'She doesn't concern you or my daughter.'

Tessa was about to question this, but then thought better of it. It would only start another row. So she sipped more wine and that made things feel better.

He looked uncomfortable again. For a man who seemed absolutely certain of his own rightness, this was a bit surprising. Eventually he said, 'I feel very awkward about asking this but I'm going to. I told you that in a fortnight I have to go to France, and circumstances mean that I have to take Lucy with me. She doesn't want to go—and I don't blame her.' He stopped, took a mouthful of wine and went on. 'Would you come with us to France as Lucy's companion? It would be an entirely business arrangement—I would pay you. And you might even enjoy it.'

'Not a chance!' The answer was out before she could think about it. 'Now, are you going to threaten to sue me again?'

'No. Neither am I going to try to persuade you. I'll just pour you a little more wine and ask you to think about it.'

So he poured the wine and she thought. She thought it was excellent wine. 'Yesterday you were threatening me. Today you're asking me for a favour. You know you're hardly my idea of my favourite man.'

'I can believe that. Surprisingly, you are my idea of my favourite companion for my daughter. Having you along would please her no end, and that would please me.'

'I like Lucy but I'm still not sure about you. Why should I help you?'

Tessa put down her glass and looked at it in amazement. What was in it, a truth drug? Had she just said that? To the man who was to be her new boss?

But he laughed. 'I can understand you not thinking much of me and I can live with it. But I know you're a good A and E nurse and I think you'd like to help Lucy. And you know this would help her.'

Tessa felt herself being gradually being worked into a corner. She tried to fight back, be provocative. 'Going abroad with you? Neither of us married? What would people think?'

He wasn't to be provoked. 'What would people think?' he said irritably. 'They'd think the truth, that you're a very good choice on my part as a companion for my daughter. Any suggestion of anything between us would be…ridiculous.'

That's not very flattering, she thought.

And then, perhaps, he thought the same. He went on, 'And even if we were…attracted to one another, I would suggest for Lucy's sake that we keep our distance. You've got to get to know her.'

'I think we like each other,' Tessa said.

'Perhaps so, and I'm very pleased.' He frowned. 'So what do you say?'

Tessa stood. 'I haven't made up my mind yet. But if you don't mind I'll go and see what Lucy feels about me going with you.'

'A good idea.'

Being a teenager, Lucy wasn't going to admit to any real enthusiasm. 'All right, if you want to,' she said with elaborate unconcern. 'It's fine by me.'

So Tessa went back to the study and said, 'I'd like to go with you. If it can be arranged with the department.'

'I'm very pleased and I'm sure it can be arranged. We go a fortnight tomorrow, setting off on Sunday night and coming back on Wednesday. That OK by you?'

'Fine,' she said, wondering what she'd let herself in for. And why, for that matter.

'Then how about another glass of wine?'

'Actually, I think I'd better go home,' she said.

As she drove home she wondered why, exactly, she had agreed to go to France with James Armstrong and his daughter. Certainly she liked Lucy and was looking forward to going to France, but she had to admit that it was the prospect of seeing more of the father that was making her heart beat faster.

CHAPTER THREE

TESSA wasn't at work for the next three days, and returned to duty on Wednesday morning when she was on earlies—seven in the morning until two in the afternoon.

She was just finishing bandaging the knee of Joe Black, a wide-eyed nine-year-old who said nothing, didn't flinch, but hung firmly onto the hand of his mother. Tessa had been told that Joe had been too eager to go to school. He had bounded out of the car, tripped on the pavement and fallen onto a piece of broken glass. Tessa wondered about the people who would drop bottles outside a primary school but that wasn't her concern. Very sensibly, Joe's mother had driven him straight to the hospital.

The knee had been X-rayed and no glass fragments were left in it. Jack had stitched the wound and Tessa was finishing the dressing.

Joe's white-faced mother was holding him on her knee and Tessa wondered if she was in need of medical treatment, too.

'All finished, and you've been a very brave little boy,' Tessa said. 'I think that deserves a badge.' From a drawer she took a large yellow smiley sticker, and stuck it on the front of Joe's jumper. Joe bent his head to study it. Then, for the first time, he smiled.

'I'll get you a cup of tea,' Tessa said to Mrs Black. 'Sit and drink it before you go home. You feel all right to drive?'

'I'll be OK,' the woman said. 'You know, I've always hated the sight of blood, it used to make me sick. But when I saw Joe bleeding so badly I knew I had to cope on my own, and I did.'

'Sometimes people here surprise themselves with what they can do when they have to. Now, you take Joe to the waiting room and I'll fetch you that drink.'

On her way back from the waiting room she saw a white-coated figure come out of a cubicle. The figure had his back to her, but with a shock she recognised the broad shoulders and longish dark hair. James Armstrong. Well, she'd known that in time she'd see him at work. Why should the sight of him make her heart beat a little faster? They weren't enemies any more. It was just a bit of a shock, she decided.

He turned and saw her. 'Good morning, Nurse Calvert. We meet—professionally—at last.' For once he didn't scowl, but allowed himself a small smile. It made his face much more attractive.

'Mr Armstrong,' she said with a bright, professional smile. 'I hope you're finding everything to your satisfaction.'

He frowned. 'Not everything. There are a few things here and there that I want to change, I'll be having a meeting about it later. Tell me, in this department are you always so formal? No first names used at all?'

Tessa giggled, she couldn't help it. 'People will call you "sir" because they're a bit unsure, a bit frightened of you. It's up to you to set the tone. And nobody called Mr Pell anything but "sir". He trained at a time when all consultants thought they were gods.'

'Some of them still think they are,' he muttered. 'Miss Calvert—Tessa—I'd like the senior nursing staff at least to call me by my first name. Except if a situation calls for formality.'

'Of course,' said Tessa demurely. 'Pleased to meet you, James.' She held out her hand. 'Or, since we're going to be friends, should I call you Jimmy?'

His eyes sparked with amusement. 'No! No, no, no, no. I hate Jimmy. Call me Jimmy and that's it. You wouldn't like—'

The triage nurse hurried up to them. 'Mr Armstrong, there's an RTA just come in, if you're not too busy.'

James turned to Tessa. 'Let's see how we work together,' he said.

Of course the woman wasn't an RTA, that was a statistic. This was a person. Tessa walked into the cubicle and smiled at the woman lying on the bed. For a moment James stayed outside and had a muttered conversation with the paramedics who had brought the woman in.

The patient was a well-dressed woman of about forty, awkwardly clutching a bloodstained pad to the right side of her head with her left hand. Her right arm lay by her side. She was conscious. 'I feel an utter fool,' she said to Tessa. 'I'm a solicitor, I have my own practice. People like me don't walk into the road without looking.'

'People like you can do all sorts of foolish things sometimes,' Tessa said gently. 'We all do. Now, I'm Staff Nurse Tessa Calvert. I need to take a few details, then we'll get you sorted out.' She reached for a notepad.

It was drummed into all A and E nurses. If it was

at all possible, take personal details and a history before doing anything. Fortunately this woman was very clear-headed. If anything, she seemed irritated rather than in pain.

First, name, address, any current medical problems, family or who to contact. 'Do you want me to send for anyone? Family, husband or partner?'

'Thank you, no. Though I'd appreciate it if someone could phone my firm and tell them where I am.'

Tessa promised to see to it. 'Can you tell me what happened?'

'I was walking to work, I always do. At the moment I have a bit of a problem case, a child-custody appeal. I'm representing the father and things are difficult. Anyway, I was thinking of this as I crossed the road where I always cross—and I didn't look. A bus knocked me over. I was carried into the nearest shop, which was a newsagent's, and shortly afterwards the ambulance arrived. I feel such a fool!'

James appeared by the bedside. 'Hi,' he said, with a warm smile that made Tessa's heart miss a beat. 'I'm James Armstrong, the consultant here. Tessa and I are going to get you sorted out as quickly as we can. And you are…?'

The patient was pale through shock, but Tessa was half-amused to see a faint trace of colour appear on her cheekbones. James had had an effect already— though not a medical one.

'Annabel Knight. Pleased to meet you, Doctor. I— Ow!' Annabel tried to offer her hand to shake then thought better of it. It hurt to move her arm.

James gently pressed the arm down. 'Don't try to move, Annabel.' His hand felt for the pulse in Annabel's wrist, and Tessa knew he was checking all the other signs—breathing, involuntary movements, size of the irises.

He snapped on a pair of rubber gloves, then he gently moved Annabel's hand from the side of her face and peered at the gash underneath.

'I think this looks much worse than it really is. We'll have to suture it, of course, but I'm pretty sure I can do it without leaving much of a scar. How's your arm feel?'

'It feels broken,' Annabel said flatly.

'A very accurate diagnosis. Now I'll just give you a quick once-over and then Tessa here will help you get undressed and we'll have a closer look at you. Everything's going to be fine, Annabel.'

'No, it's not. I'm missing a morning's work.'

But Annabel's toughness was running out and a moment later her eyes fluttered shut. She wasn't unconscious but she wouldn't want to talk for a while.

With Tessa's help James checked her pulse, took the blood pressure, temperature, noted the respirations and examined the pupils for signs of concussion. All seemed well. Then he left Tessa to undress the patient.

Annabel's eyes flickered open. 'How are you going to get this jacket off me without hurting my arm?'

'We'll have to cut it,' said Tessa. 'Otherwise you might really suffer.'

'I am suffering. This suit cost me two hundred pounds. All right, cut away.'

Annabel knew she had broken her arm and gashed her face, but thought that was all. Tessa and James knew that might not be the case. It was possible for patients to have quite serious injuries and know nothing of them. So when James returned he conducted a careful examination. But Annabel was fine. The arm and head were X-rayed on a portable machine, and while they waited for the films Tessa bathed the head wound, cleaned and irrigated it. James came and peered over her shoulder. 'We'll have to shave a little of your head, Annabel,' he said, 'but we'll keep it to the minimum.'

'Whatever is necessary.'

Tessa wished that all their patients were as co-operative as this one.

Next, James sutured the gash. Tessa watched. She had seen many doctors and surgeons do this. Most were competent, some were a bit clumsy, some were good. But James was brilliant! He pulled the split flesh together, aligned it perfectly, kept exactly the right amount of tension on the thread. She knew what he'd said was true—there wouldn't be much of a scar when he had finished.

And all the time he worked he kept up a conversation with the patient until finally it was done. James stripped off his gloves, went to look at the X-rays that had just been delivered. He winced.

'What d'you think, Tessa?'

Tessa studied the black and white images. A comminuted fracture of the humerus—she could see the bone splinters.

'Beyond us. Annabel needs to be admitted to Orthopaedics.'

'I agree. I'll phone for someone to come down to look at her.'

He turned, smiled down at the recumbent body. 'Annabel, I'm going to arrange for you to be sent up to a ward where someone can deal with this arm. You need specialist care. But don't worry, all will be well.'

'Thank you, Doctor, thank you for everything. You've been very good.'

James left. Thoughtfully, Annabel said, 'He *was* very good, wasn't he? He'd make a good solicitor, he can deal with people.'

'Yes, he can,' said Tessa thoughtfully. Working with James had been a revelation. There was a side to his character she had never suspected. She had known he would be technically good, but he was good at handling people, too. A vast improvement on Francis Pell, who thought that people were just an awkward means of manifesting injuries. Maybe she would have to review her ideas about James.

In fact, James returned two minutes later with the junior orthopaedics registrar. While they were looking at the X-rays Jack appeared, white-faced. 'If you have a moment, James, we've got a SIDS coming in.'

'Right. We've finished here.' James and Tessa said a quick goodbye to Annabel and walked out of the cubicle.

SIDS. Sudden infant death syndrome. Tessa had only been present at one before, it was an experience she had never wanted to repeat. No one really knew the cause. Perhaps five hundred children, usually between the ages of two and six months, died of it each year. A perfectly healthy child—and a few hours later he or she was dead. It was traumatic for medical staff as well as for parents.

The little boy was hurried into Resus and a desperate attempt made to revive him. But when they saw the limp body everyone there knew that there was no hope at all. The mother sat in the corner of the room, her body rigid, her hands clutching tightly at the seat of her chair. She wouldn't be moved, she would answer no questions. She sat there, staring at the brightly illuminated table and the white-clad figures round it, as if the sheer intensity of her gaze might help.

James did all that was possible. Eventually he looked round the table, waited for the nods of all concerned. All attempts at resuscitation would now cease. There was no point.

James walked to the still figure of the mother and gently said, 'We've done all that we can, Mrs Williams. I'm so sorry, but I'm afraid that we weren't able to resuscitate Michael.'

Then the pent-up emotions burst out and the mother howled in anguish and buried her face in the front of James's jacket. He helped her from the room. Tessa knew that this frenzied weeping was the best possible thing for the mother, but it hurt everyone else. One by one the other staff drifted out.

As senior nurse there, Tessa knew the body was her concern. The little boy must be washed and dressed so that his mother could hold him for the last time. She might want photographs of him.

Tessa looked at Sally, assessed the horror on her face. This was something Sally ought to do. All nurses had to get used to death, and handling bodies, as quickly as possible. But a baby was different. Tessa decided to prepare the body herself. There were other things Sally could do.

In time it was done. The husband and the parish priest had been sent for, they had taken the mother away. There were procedures for this kind of occurrence. It happened, the work of the department had to go on.

But Tessa couldn't go on. She was entitled to a

break, she was going to take it. So she went to the little lounge. Fortunately it was empty. She sat there—and let the tears run down her face.

Ten minutes later Jack and James entered. Jack came over, hugged her quickly and said he would pour her a drink. As he moved to the coffee-machine she felt James studying her.

'We're medical staff, Tessa,' he said quietly. 'We can't afford the luxury of tears, they aren't necessary. You must remain detached. You can't afford emotion.'

'Perhaps you can't afford emotion. I can. If I can't feel for people I'm no good as a nurse.'

'Just so long as you don't let your emotions get in the way of the smooth running of my department.' Then he was gone.

After drinking half of the truly terrible coffee Jack had given her she felt a little better, and also a little angry. 'Can't afford emotion! He can't afford emotion but I can! I know that he's a really good doctor but he's too hard. He just has no feelings at all.'

'Perhaps,' said Jack. 'Or he might have feelings and be just too scared of giving way to them.'

'I doubt that.'

It was good of Jack to sit there with her, to try to cheer her a little, to leave his arms round her in what was definitely a brotherly way. It was good to have someone there. Ten minutes later the door banged open and James peered round it.

'Dr Harris, you're an SHO in an A and E department, not a sister of mercy offering comfort to the afflicted. If you can spare the time, I need your assistance.'

'Coming at once.' The door banged shut as Jack hurried after him.

Tessa stared, open-mouthed, after the two.

Half an hour later she had recovered. She was working with Jack, helping him with some of the interminable forms he had to fill in. 'Sorry I was the cause of you getting into trouble,' she said when they had nearly finished, 'but I was glad you were there.'

'Glad to be of help,' said Jack amiably. 'And James didn't mention it. We were fine working together.'

Tessa's voice was tentative. 'D'you think he was right, shouting at you like that? Was it necessary?'

Jack shrugged. 'He's starting a new job, he takes it very seriously. But he does seem a bit strung out, he needs to relax somehow. I gather he has a daughter but no wife or partner. Perhaps he needs the love of a good woman.'

Lucky woman, Tessa thought privately.

Of course, she knew more about James and his daughter than Jack did. But the man was still an enigma. Who was Lucy's mother? Why had an obviously good-looking man like James never married again? Well, that was none of her business. But something James had said definitely was her business.

It was nearly the end of her shift before she managed to catch James when he wasn't working. Unlike the previous consultant, who'd thought his job had been to maintain just an overview, James seemed ever ready to get involved. Difficult, when she wanted a private word with him. But at last she found her chance.

'James, d'you think I could have a talk with you—in private? It shouldn't take long.'

He looked at her thoughtfully. 'We'll go to my room.'

It was only a small room, and after the filing cabinets, desk and two chairs had been crammed in there wasn't much space for two people. She was alarmingly close to him, and their legs kept on meeting under the desk.

'So, Tessa, what can I do for you?'

She hadn't rehearsed what she was going to say, perhaps that was a mistake. But she knew she had to say something. 'Earlier on you told me to remain detached, that I couldn't afford emotion. You suggested that being emotional would affect my work as a nurse.'

'More or less,' he agreed. 'We can't have tears when we need action.'

'Have you any complaints about my work as a nurse this morning?'

'None at all. I am not trying to compliment you when I say that your work is exceptional.'

The funny thing, she realised, was that he meant it. He wasn't trying to compliment her. It was just a dispassionate observation.

She took a deep breath. 'I regard my...emotional input...as being vital to my work. Without that I'm just a mechanic. I could be working with machines, not human beings.'

James nodded. 'All medical staff—doctors, nurses, orderlies, technicians—must recognise that they are dealing with human beings, and treat their patients with the utmost courtesy. I'm sure we agree on that.'

'Oh, we do! But there's so much more. You must feel to be a nurse.'

'You must also think. In my time I've seen sloppy,

emotional nurses and doctors who think that because they feel for their patients, they are doing them some good. And often the opposite is the case.'

She had nothing to say to this, she knew there was a touch of truth in what he said.

'Tessa, I'm sorry if I upset you with my remark, but you're likely to hear something like that again. I do think you're a great asset to this department. I was also thinking that in some way...we could come to be friends.'

'Friends?'

They stared at each other, and once again she felt that weird sense of togetherness they had both experienced the first time they met. It unsettled her and she knew it unsettled him, too.

'Friends—or something like that.' His beeper sounded. He stood, obviously relieved. 'I'm needed. I must go, Tessa.'

She had to stand to let him out and for a moment they were inches apart, face to face. 'I'd like to be your friend, too, James. But don't try to fool me, or yourself. Somewhere inside you there's emotion. You might think you've got it under control but one day it'll amaze you and burst out. I hope no one near gets burned.'

'Tessa, I have to go,' he said. His voice was slightly uneven.

Letters to Tessa's programme were sent to the radio station and when she came off shift she drove round to pick up any more that had arrived. On the receptionist's desk was a bunch of flowers in a vase, a variety of sweet peas. Tessa bent over to smell them.

'They're for you,' June said. 'Brought in this morning. I put them in water to keep them fresh. I'll wrap them in some newspaper when you go.'

'For me! Who from?'

'A girl. With a baby in a pram. I think she was a satisfied customer.'

'That's lovely! I've had letters saying thank you but this is the first time anyone has sent me anything.'

'This card was attached to the flowers,' June said, handing it over.

Tessa took out a card. 'Thank you. No one else listened, but you did. It felt so good to know that somebody cared.' She read the little message again. Was there a sense of desperation there? She showed the card to June and asked, 'What was she like, this girl who brought in the flowers?'

June was obviously choosing her words with care. 'She was youngish—I doubt any more than twenty. And she looked tired. I told her to take a handful of those sweets that we leave on the counter, and she did. No wedding ring but, of course, these days that means nothing.'

'How was she dressed?'

Again, June chose her words with care. 'Her clothes were clean but they'd seen better days. The baby was better dressed—but the pushchair was a bit battered.'

'And she didn't leave her name or anything?'

'No. I asked her to but she said it didn't matter.'

Tessa took the flowers and the card home with her. After she had opened all the other letters and drafted replies on her PC, she cleared her desk and put the little card in the centre. She reread it. Was it desperation she could detect?

The note was handwritten, using a thin black ballpoint. The writing was neat, instantly legible. Tessa clipped it to her writing stand and then turned to her files.

Like all nurses, she had a horror of lost or badly kept files. Each letter she had received was filed in date order. Stapled to it was a copy of the reply she had sent and a note of any leaflets that she might have enclosed. She had a great store of leaflets, dealing with everything from pregnancy to housing benefit.

Now she flicked through the letters she had received over the past three weeks. And there was one from a fortnight ago—written in the same hand, with the same pen but this time with a name. The girl was called Anita Barnes.

She hadn't read the letter out on the radio. But her reply had been a bit longer than usual, possibly because the girl's story might have been her own. It wasn't an unusual story.

Anita had been brought up by an aunt in the Isle of Wight. Her childhood hadn't been too happy as the aunt hadn't really understood children. Then Anita had met a man who had wanted her to move to the north with him. The aunt had not been very happy with this. They'd had a fight and Anita had left, vowing never to return. The rest of the story was horribly convincing. The man had lost his job just as Anita had found that she was pregnant. He'd drunk, taken drugs and eventually he'd left her. Now Anita was left in a dank council flat with only just enough to live on, no friends and no prospect of a job. She could cope—just. But apart from watching little Sylvia grow up, there seemed little in life to look forward to.

Tessa sighed as she reread her reply. It seemed a

bit facile now, but she was glad it had been of use to
Anita. She wrote down the address on a piece of pa-
per. She'd think about the girl, at least send her another note thanking her for the flowers.

That night Tessa rang Lucy. Fortunately James wasn't
there. After this afternoon she thought she'd better
keep a low profile for a while.

'Lucy, I'm thinking of making you the subject of
my talk this coming Friday. Specifically, I'm going
to talk about lying—or at any rate not telling the full
truth. You won't be mentioned by name, of course,
but do you mind?'

As ever, Lucy started by being offhand. 'I guess
not. I guess I deserve it.' Then she giggled. 'Fancy
me being the subject of a radio talk.'

'You're not the subject! You're just the peg I'm
going to hang a few remarks on.'

'Sure, sure. Listen, Tessa, what are you going to
wear for our trip to France? I asked Dad and all he
could say was don't wear anything too outrageous. I
suppose he means don't wear anything that will let
him down.'

'Well, you don't want to let him down, do you?'

Tessa thought for a moment. 'For a start, it'll probably be hotter than here so take at least a couple of
flowing summer dresses. And something a bit formal
for dinner—not shorts.'

'I doubt we'll be going out to dinner, but OK.'

'Have you got a hat to wear in the sun? A straw
one perhaps?'

'I was made to wear a beret at my last school. I
vowed never to wear a hat again.'

'Well, perhaps we'll shop for one there. You'll

need it in the heat. And I gather we're travelling by car. It'll be a long journey, so wear something comfortable.'

'That's good. Thanks, Tessa.'

That was advice a mother would have given, Tessa thought as she rang off. A pity Lucy apparently didn't have one.

'So no matter how strongly you feel, covering up the truth is never going to help. In the long run it can only make things worse. Remember, you can always talk. And remember also that talking includes listening. You'd be surprised at the number of problems that can be solved if both parties are honest and willing to listen. Got any problems? Why not ''Ask A Nurse''?'

'That was good,' said Ray, 'but they're all good. How are you getting on with this fellow anyway? Is he a good boss?'

She'd already told Ray there was no need to worry about being sued. He'd been very relieved.

'He's not a bad boss,' she said. 'I think I'm getting through to him. We agree on quite a few things now.'

CHAPTER FOUR

SATURDAY night was party night! Tessa found herself looking forward to it. Jack had told her that they'd be going with another couple, a young doctor and his wife, and that he'd arranged for them to be at a big table with several other couples. Just what she needed. She knew she was good in large groups—it was the one-to-one situations that caused trouble for her.

And she liked dancing. She found a dress that was simple but elegant, and brushed out her hair till it hung to her shoulders. She wanted to look good.

She was picked up in a taxi by Jack and the other couple and driven to the hospital social club. It was a good club, with a sprung dance floor and tables down each side. They bought a round of drinks and found their table. She was going to enjoy herself.

Tessa knew practically everyone at their table and there were many friends and colleagues at other tables. She never seemed to stop dancing. Half of the time she danced with Jack. Perhaps he drank just a little too much, perhaps he held her a bit too close. But, then, he was a friend. She knew there'd be no trouble with Jack.

There was a break from the dancing while they ate from the plates of finger food placed on the table. 'Look who's just come in,' someone said.

She looked. There was James, looking every inch the consultant in a dark suit, white shirt and college tie. With him was Lucy. She was wearing a long and probably expensive dress that Tessa thought far too old for her. She was scowling. They joined the table of another couple. Tessa recognised them as Harry Jowett and his wife—he was the hospital consultant haematologist and she a ward sister.

'If that's Armstrong's daughter, she doesn't look as if she's having a very good time,' one of her table companions said.

'Would you if you were at that table?' someone else asked.

Then the music started again and Tessa went to dance with Jack.

When the dance ended and they were walking back, Tessa glanced at the Armstrongs' table. The two men and the wife were deep in some kind of discussion—almost certainly medical, Tessa guessed. And Lucy was sitting with her head down, with no one to talk to and obviously bored.

Tessa hesitated a moment, nerved herself then walked over to their table. She smiled at the group there and said to James, 'May Lucy come over and sit with us?'

James looked alarmed but Lucy nodded, hopefully. 'May I, Dad? I certainly can't join in this conversation.'

'We are boring, aren't we?' Harry Jowett said with a grin.

James looked at Tessa thoughtfully. 'All right, Lucy,' he said, 'but if you have a drink, remember, only wine and water.'

'I'll stick to Coke. Come on, Tessa, let's go.'

'You surprised him,' she whispered to Tessa as

they walked back. 'He wasn't expecting that and he doesn't like surprises. He likes to be in control.'

'That's my boss you're talking about. He's supposed to be in control.'

Lucy was shy and quiet at first, but Jack fetched her a Coke and after a while she was deep in conversation with a couple of the younger nurses. Then Tessa danced with a doctor friend of Jack's and enjoyed herself immensely. Suddenly the doctor said, 'Well, will you look at that?' He put his hands on Tessa's waist, gently turned her round.

Lucy was dancing with a trainee nurse, an amiable young man called Sean, who sported spiky, dyed blond hair. It was obvious that Sean fancied himself as a bit of a dancer. It was equally obvious that Lucy was much better than him. But Sean wasn't going to give up easily. Whatever Lucy could do, he could do, too, so the dance turned into a fierce but friendly competition. At the end the surrounding dancers clapped them both.

After that Tessa was pleased to see that Lucy was one of the group. Her scowl had gone and she looked the eager-faced, attractive young girl that she was.

And then someone behind Tessa said, 'Excuse me.' She turned, and there was James. 'May I dance with you?' he asked.

She had never expected this. Unable to speak, she offered him her arm and he led her onto the floor. Fortunately the music had switched to ballroom style. She couldn't have envisaged gyrating opposite him as she had so happily before with the other doctor. Neither could she imagine him dancing in that style. Far too abandoned for him.

It was a good thing too in that he had to lead. She

couldn't have...what was she thinking about! He was only a man! But what a man.

His arm was firm round her waist. Like Jack, he held her close—but this time she rather liked it. He was a skilful dancer, which surprised her. Perhaps, like his daughter, he had a natural sense of rhythm.

She was enjoying herself. She could smell his expensive aftershave, feel the warmth and grip of his hand round hers. When an over-enthusiastic couple blundered near them, his arms tightened round her waist and he swung her effortlessly away. And after a while they started to chat.

'It was good of you to invite Lucy to your table,' he said. 'It was just what she needed and I didn't think of it.'

'You're a father,' Tessa teased. 'Why should you know what she wants? I'm a girl, like Lucy, and we enjoy the same things.'

'Like dancing—even with me?'

'Don't fish for compliments. You're a very good dancer—as I suspect you know.'

'Thank you. I did a lot of dancing—once.' This was said in a totally different tone, but Tessa decided not to probe. Well, not just yet.

The danced ended. Like a Jane Austen heroine, she swept him a curtsy and, like Darcy, he bowed stiffly from the waist. Then he took her hand to escort her back to her table.

'I'd forgotten what fun dancing was. Do you think I should really embarrass Lucy and ask her to dance?'

Tessa glanced at the glowing Lucy, surrounded by her new friends. 'No,' she said.

'I entirely agree. And it would be improper for me to ask you to dance again. You are with Jack.'

'Just for tonight! There's nothing serious between us, we're just...we're just friends.'

'I see. Yes, I did enjoy dancing with you.' He hesitated. 'Do you think perhaps some time, not tonight, we might dance together again?'

'I'd like that,' she said. He was still holding her hand and, impulsively, she squeezed it. He squeezed hers back.

She laughed, rather uncertainly. 'Squeezing hands. You make me feel like a schoolgirl again,' she said.

'Whatever we are, we aren't schoolchildren, Tessa. People like us don't bounce in and out of relationships like Lucy.'

Relationships? The thought of having a relationship with James made her feel inexplicably excited and scared at the same time.

He saw her to her seat, then stayed for a couple of minutes longer, chatting to Jack and the rest of the staff there. Tessa could see how absolutely charming he was. After a while he excused himself and went back to his friends. And five minutes later three opened bottles of wine were set on the table. 'With the compliments of Mr Armstrong.'

'Your dad said you could have a glass of wine and water,' Tessa said to Lucy. 'Do you want to have some now?'

Lucy shook her head. 'I'll pick up brownie points if I stick to Coke for now. But thanks for asking. Tessa, I've got something to ask you, a favour.'

'Go on,' Tessa said cautiously.

'Well, I've started at this new school. I'm all right with it, I'm fitting in. But you're expected to do some kind of public service. You know, help the old or the young or the sick or the environment or something. I wondered if I could do anything in A and E? Perhaps work with you?'

Tessa considered. 'What does your dad say?'

'I haven't asked him. This was something I wanted to organise on my own.'

'Well, the first thing we'd have to do is get his permission. It's his department. And then there's all sorts of insurance questions. But I'll certainly look into it for you.' She looked at the young girl. 'And A and E is tough.'

'I know. I live with my dad, I can see what effect it has on him sometimes—it gets to him.'

That interested Tessa. So James wasn't as hard as he pretended to be. 'Well, what I'll do first is ask your dad if you can shadow me for a day. Then we'll take it from there.'

'Great! But not for a few weeks yet. There's some music I've got to get on top of first.'

Tessa was working the next day. Sunday often wasn't too busy. She knew James was in as she had seen him arrive, although he wasn't down on the roster to be on duty. Probably catching up on paperwork. When she had a quiet moment she knocked on his office door.

'Tessa, good to see you! Now, is this a professional or a personal visit?'

When he smiled his entire face changed. She thought he spent far too much of his time scowling. 'Personal, I guess. But your person, not mine.'

'Sounds interesting. Sit down, if you can, and we'll chat.' Once again they were to play footsie under his tiny desk. 'What about my person, then?'

'In fact, your daughter's person. She asked if she

would be able to do some voluntary work in A and
E with me, so I wonder if she could come in one day
and shadow me? Then, if she liked it, we could arrange for her to do that voluntary work here.'

'Why did she ask you and not me?'

'She wanted to do something on her own. She
wants to be independent.'

James thought about this. 'That's good. I have no
objections to it—so long as she doesn't try to trade
on who I am. Will you look into it, see what can be
done?'

'I'd be happy to.'

He looked at her thoughtfully. 'We seem to have
come a long way since I yelled at you in that pub.
You're getting to be a part of my life. I didn't expect
this.'

Tessa tried not to show any of the mixed-up emotions she was feeling. 'We work together and I've got
an interest in Lucy. That's all it is.'

'Is it? I wonder if that's true. I know I shouldn't
say this to a nurse in my department, but I find myself
thinking about you quite a lot.'

Tessa's bleeper sounded. She sat without moving
until James drily said, 'Hadn't you better answer it?'

So she did and she had to leave at once. 'We'll
finish our conversation later,' he said, and she wondered what he might want to say to her.

It was only a small emergency but Tessa was soon
absorbed in her work. Five-year-old Melanie had broken or sprained her wrist. Jack and another nurse were
dealing with her and the little girl was surprisingly
calm. But Melanie had been brought in by her young
nanny Hilde, who spoke little English. She made up
for it by being emotional. Eventually Tessa got a

home telephone number out of her. Melanie's mother was as calm as Hilde was excitable. She arrived in ten minutes, gave permission for the X-rays and pacified Hilde, as Jack strapped up Melanie's arm. This was often the case in A and E. For the time being Tessa's conversation with James was forgotten.

She walked into the corridor—and there he was, beckoning her. But this wasn't the pleasant man she'd chatted to three quarters of an hour ago. He was white-faced with anger.

'Tessa, will you go into cubicle six and supervise Nurse Kent? Or perhaps you'd better do the work yourself. We have a seven-year-old child there, suffering from an acute asthma attack, possibly brought on by emotional factors. I've prescribed an aerosol bronchodilator. He may also need oxygen.'

Tessa looked at him in horror. 'I certainly will, James. There is no way a first-year nurse should... You didn't ask her to?'

'Of course I didn't! Any possible emergency would be far beyond her capacities. But she's made a reasonable job so far, so perhaps it's best if she carries on. Cubicle six, Tessa!'

Tessa hurried down the corridor to cubicle six to find Sally. Quickly Tessa checked. The child was sitting forward and the nebuliser kept upright. As James had said, Sally had made quite a reasonable job so far. But no way should she have been left on her own!

When there was a convenient moment she pulled Sally to one side, 'What happened, Sally?'

'Mr Armstrong came in. He was ever so angry, I could tell, but not at me, though. He looked at Sammy here and then walked out saying he'd find someone to help me.'

'Why are you doing this? You're not trained for it yet.'

'Fay Roberts started but asked me to carry on. She said she'd had no lunch and she'd had a hard time at the party last night and desperately needed a drink. There didn't seem to be any senior doctors around so off she went. And I did the best I could.'

'I see,' said Tessa. 'Well, basically all we have to do is wait. Sammy might need oxygen. But if you give him too much you could stop spontaneous respiration. This is because…'

Twenty minutes Sammy seemed to be much better. But, Tessa cautioned Sally, this often happened just before complete respiratory failure. They both looked into the corridor to see if there was a doctor handy.

James was standing in the middle of the corridor, arms folded, legs apart. Tessa could only see the back of him, but from the way his head was hunched forward she could guess exactly what his expression was. James was angry and it showed.

Further down the corridor they saw Fay Roberts approaching. They saw her see James, hesitate and then turn as if to walk into the sluice room.

'Staff Nurse Roberts, come here!'

James's furious voice echoed down the corridor. Fay stopped, wavered and then walked slowly forward.

'You wanted me, Mr Armstrong?' She tried to pretend that nothing was the matter, but her pretence fooled no one.

Now James's voice was soft, and that made it even more frightening than ever. He waved Sally forward. 'I found this trainee nurse performing a task that I specifically asked you to do. Nurse Kent is neither trained nor qualified to perform that task. Quite possibly one of my patients might have been put at risk. Why weren't you doing your job?'

Fay tried to fight back. 'That child will be fine. I've been working all day without a break. I'm entitled to a lunch-break and—'

'Don't tell me that child will be fine! No good nurse would leave a patient at risk to have a lunch-break. I've noticed your behaviour before and asked that you be cautioned. Apparently you've ignored that warning. Now, go and tell the ward manager that I won't have you working for me. Ever!'

'You can't do that. I—'

'Oh, yes I can! Don't push me, Staff Nurse Roberts, or you'll find exactly what I can and cannot do. Now, get out of my sight!'

James watched as Fay turned and stumbled back down the corridor. Then he turned to Sally. 'You were doing very well when I saw you and I was most impressed. But remember in future, if anyone asks—or tells—you to do something that you feel unsure about, check with a senior member of staff. OK?'

'Y-Yes, sir,' Sally stammered.

James strode off down the corridor. Sally looked at Tessa, who shrugged.

'I didn't realise he could be as hard as that,' Sally said, 'but he was fair to me.'

'Yes, he was,' said Tessa. 'Hard but fair. It's an unsettling combination.'

Gossip spread fast in a department like A and E. Within half an hour everyone knew what had happened, from nurses to consultants to cleaners. That afternoon—when everyone was certain that James had gone home—five of the nurses and junior doctors managed to collect in the coffee-room and discuss it.

The general opinion was that James had gone a bit far. But everyone there knew that Fay had been getting away with things for far too long. The old consultant had been too soft on her, and had made rather a favourite of her as they had worked together many years previously.

A young house officer said, 'I was on nights last week and a bit out of my depth. Mr Armstrong was on call, sleeping at the hospital. I had to call him out three times and each time he came there was nothing much wrong. But he never blamed me. You work for him and he'll work for you. This place is going to benefit from him being here.'

Tessa wondered if she, too, would benefit from working with James. And if so, how?

Perhaps it was a silly thing to do. As a nurse Tessa knew how dangerous it could be to get involved in her patients' private lives, and the same went for the troubled people who wrote to her radio show for advice. She had to be sympathetic, but ultimately detached. Otherwise how would she cope with the next one? Yes, it was silly—but she thought she'd just call in.

Anita Barnes lived in a small council flat in a tower block on the outskirts of town. It wasn't a bad neighbourhood—it was a nothing neighbourhood. It was soulless. But the windows of the flat sparkled and the curtains had been recently washed. Anita was making an effort.

It was a warm evening and the door was half-open.

Tessa tapped hesitantly then called, 'Hello? Is Anita Barnes in?'

Seconds later the door was thrown open and a thin girl in T-shirt and shorts beamed at Tessa. 'I recognised your voice. You're the nurse from *Ask A Nurse*. Tessa Calvert. I listen to you every Friday. I look forward to it. It's lovely to see you. Will you come in?'

Tessa stepped inside, squeezed round the pram in the hall and was led into the tiny sitting room. She sat on the couch, an old one judging by the state of the springs but made attractive by a bright red throw.

'You called and left me some flowers.' She smiled. 'I'm sorry I wasn't there so I called round to say thank you. I'm not used to getting presents like that. In fact, you're the first person ever to leave anything.'

Anita coloured. 'I just wanted to do something personal. Lots of people have been kind—the doctors and the health visitors and the midwives and so on. But I'm still a case to them rather than a person. When you wrote to me I thought you were taking a personal interest in me. So I wanted to say thank you.' She frowned. 'How did you get my address? I didn't want to leave it in case...well, I'm sure you're very busy.'

Tessa explained how she had checked her files. Then, from a half-open door behind her she heard gurgles and little grunts which she recognised at once. 'Baby's waking up,' she said. 'May I see her?'

Anita led her into the next room. There was a hand-painted cot with a home-made mobile hanging over it. 'This is Sylvia,' she said proudly, 'my little Sylvia. She's the centre of my life now.' She kissed the baby on the forehead. 'Shall we go for a walk round the estate, darling?'

Tessa hesitated. This was difficult. It was hard to know if she was helping or intruding. Eventually she said, 'There's a family pub just down the road. Round the back there's a big garden and a veranda. Would you like to bring Sylvia and we could have a meal there? Of course, if there's something else you've got to do then…'

'I don't do anything but look after Sylvia. And I'd really love to come. It's just that…'

Tessa guessed what the problem was. Anita was short of money. 'It'll be my treat, of course,' she said. 'To be exact, it'll be the radio station's treat. I do get an expense allowance I can spend how I like.'

Anita's smile widened. 'We can have dinner in the garden,' she said.

Anita needed to talk more than she needed to eat. The two of them had a salad and then Tessa sat the baby on her lap and fed her while Anita talked. Tessa had read about how isolated a young mum could be if she didn't have family support. But she needed to talk to one to appreciate the full problem.

'I'd love a job,' Anita said, 'somewhere with a crèche perhaps. I need to get out, to meet people. I've filled in lots of forms but really there's not a lot that I can do.'

'You have no skills at all?'

'Well, I've done a bit of clerical work and I enjoyed it. But in most jobs I'm competing against seventeen-year-old girls without babies. They can do the job as well as I could. Which would you choose?'

'It's a problem,' Tessa agreed. She considered. 'There's no family at all who could help you?'

Anita's gaze dropped. 'I've only got Auntie Sylvia down on the Isle of Wight. She brought me up. But we had this fearful row when I wanted to move in with Peter. She said she never wanted to see me again and I said the same. We've not been in touch since I walked out. So she'll never be any help—why should she?'

Tessa had picked up on the name. 'You called your baby after her?'

Anita shrugged. 'It was a name. The only one I could think of at the time.'

Tessa wondered if there was more to it than that. 'Why don't you write to her? A cheerful letter, let her know how you're doing?'

'What'd be the point? It'd do no good. And I'm not going to crawl!'

'You don't have to crawl, just let her know you're alive. She must have feelings. Have you thought that she might be lonely, too?'

CHAPTER FIVE

'So you don't think you understand her. Remember, Mark, some girls find it hard to commit. Perhaps she's been hurt, perhaps she's even afraid—there could be a dozen reasons why she's keeping you at a distance. But it sounds as if there's the beginning of a relationship between you. Talk to her. Give it time, be supportive, don't press her. In time you might find that the support was worthwhile. And remember. You can always *Ask A Nurse.*'

Another Friday night broadcast ended. As Tessa slipped off the cans she felt the usual mixture of exhilaration and fatigue. This was only local radio but the thought that hundreds of people had been listening to her was quite...well, it was quite something. If she managed to get onto national radio, there might be millions listening to her. That thought was frightening.

She followed Ray out of the studio and they walked across the road together to the Black Lion. They settled in their favourite banquette and he looked at her anxiously. 'How do you feel about tomorrow, Tessa?'

'A lot better than you, I should think. Ray, stop worrying. They either offer me something or they don't. I'm still happy as a nurse.'

'You'd be good at this job, I know you would.' He smiled. 'And if you look good then I do, too.'

The next morning she was to go to Manchester to talk about the possible new programme on national radio. 'Not an interview as such,' the plummy-voiced young man had said to her on the telephone. 'We just want to get to know each other. Talk about possibilities, consider our options.'

'I'm looking forward to it,' Tessa had said, and she was. It was something different.

'Remember sitting here a fortnight ago?' she said. 'When James Armstrong came steaming in?'

Ray shivered. 'I remember. It still unnerves me when I think about him. He could have ruined all my plans for a new programme. He's a frightening man. How are you getting on with him?'

She considered. 'Pretty well, I guess. He's got a temper but he's fair. He's shaking up the department but perhaps it needed shaking up. I guess…I think I like him now.'

She didn't want to talk to Ray about her feelings for James. They were too mixed up, she wasn't sure what she thought herself. She also wasn't going to tell Ray that she was accompanying James and his daughter to France in a couple of days. Ray would only ask questions and she didn't have any convincing answers.

'If we get this programme off the ground, in a few months or so perhaps you can ask him to come in and be interviewed. Tell everyone how you first met and how he got things completely wrong.'

She shivered at the very idea. 'Don't even think about it. No way would I face that man with all of England listening to me. What if he lost his temper?'

'I guess you're right,' Ray said after a moment.

Ray drove her to Manchester next day. She was wearing what she called her interview suit—a dark grey

outfit with a longish skirt and full-length sleeves. Her
blouse was a simple white and she kept her hair in
the tight pleat she wore in the department.

'Very good,' Ray said when he surveyed her. 'You
look intelligent, professional, businesslike.'

'I thought they were supposed to be more interested
in my voice than my appearance?'

'If you look good, you feel good. You look good—
how do you feel?'

'Just a bit nervous,' she said, 'but I'll get over it.'

They found their way to an expensive office block,
were conducted by security to an equally expensive
outer office and welcomed by a glacial and expensive-
looking secretary. Would they like a coffee while they
waited?

They would, and were served their drink in china
cups. 'Bit of a change from your plastic-dispensing
machine,' Tessa said, and Ray spluttered into his cup.

'Behave yourself! We're going upmarket. Get a job
here and you'll never drink from a plastic cup again.'

'Don't count on that,' the secretary said, and suddenly became human. 'You're getting the visitors'
red-carpet treatment. It's not always like this.'

Tessa obviously had to go in on her own. At first
she was nervous, but as things progressed she relaxed.
It was a hard but fair interview—for interview it certainly was.

'So how did it go?' Ray asked when they were safely
out of the building once more and in his car.

Tessa flopped back against the seat. 'It was difficult,' she said, 'but I think I did all right. They said
that if I was offered a job I'd have to go on a training
programme. They said they couldn't tell me right then

if I was successful but I'd be receiving a letter soon and it should be a pleasant one.'

'Fantastic! Tessa, we'll make a great team!'

'A long way to go first,' she said.

She had told the interviewers that she would want to carry on with her nursing career in some form or other. They had thought this would be possible, but preferably she'd find work in Manchester.

How would she feel about leaving Halstead Hospital and the friends she had there? How would she feel about not working for James? With a shock she realised that she desperately wanted to carry on working for him.

James was fair. He wouldn't use his position to ensure that Tessa would get permission to have the three days away from work. He left it to Tessa to negotiate, and since she was known as a willing worker, there was no trouble. She was away—technically—on a three-day break. What she did in those three days was her concern.

They were to travel overnight on Sunday, stay Monday and Tuesday nights and come back during the day on Wednesday.

She worked an early shift on Sunday morning, had a couple of hours' sleep in the afternoon. Her case was packed and she held a small bag that she'd keep with her on the journey.

Without telling her father, Lucy had phoned her a couple of times to ask for more advice about clothes for the trip. Underneath the teenage coolness she was getting quite excited. Tessa was excited, too—but not for the same reasons.

Five minutes before James was due to call for her

she carried her case down to the ground floor of the block of flats in which she lived.

So far she hadn't really thought about this trip and now she began to feel slightly apprehensive. She had agreed to go to France as a companion for Lucy, not for James. It was a purely business arrangement. But they would be thrown together and she still didn't know how she would handle it. They were colleagues. She liked and respected him as someone she could work with. Could they be more than that? He had implied as much and she found the idea exciting but unsettling. This was where her thoughts shied away.

She'd meant it when she'd told Jack that she never had relationships with colleagues. But whereas Jack was only a friend, James was...James made her... He was the most exciting man she'd ever met and he made her think of things, want things that she'd long since tried to give up. Confused, she tried to think of something else.

At least they had agreed to keep some distance between them while they were in France. He had said this was for Lucy's sake. She wondered if there was another reason. Tessa knew he was feeling some of the stirrings that she was feeling herself. What would he want to do about them?

James was on time, to the minute. She might have guessed the kind of car he would have. It was a sports car, highly polished and burgundy in colour. He stepped out of the car, hurried across to take the case from her and stowed it in the boot. He was wearing a pair of dark jeans and a loose blue long-sleeved T-shirt. Whatever he wore he looked good in, she thought.

'I hope you don't mind sitting in the front,' he said,

'though you can recline the seat if you wish. I've made Lucy a nest in the back so she can sleep.'

'I'm not going to sleep in the back,' came a voice. 'I have to keep an eye on the driver.'

'Tessa will keep an eye on me,' James said agreeably. 'Won't you, Tessa?'

'I certainly will.' She buckled herself in and the car slid smoothly forward. 'There is one thing, James. I've got an advanced driver's certificate and my insurance covers me for all cars. It would make sense if I drove some of the way. Or are you one of those men who treat their cars as if they were their children? Who think women can't drive?'

'I've always found women to be much safer drivers than men, and a lot more calming to be with. I'd be delighted if you'd do some of the driving. How about if I do the first couple of hours?'

'As you wish.' Secretly, she was pleased that he was going to let her get behind the wheel of his car. She'd thought he'd be the kind of man to think that only he was fit to drive. He had surprised her—again.

It didn't surprise her to discover that he was a very good driver himself. He was fast and decisive but not aggressive. They moved quickly out of town and were soon on the motorway, heading south.

'We could have flown to France,' he said after a while, 'or even taken the train to Lille and then changed. But I've always loved driving. There's nothing like getting up, knowing that you'll soon be on the road to some distant destination. Especially abroad. Have you ever driven in America?'

'Never been there, always wanted to.'

'There's a road that crosses Nevada that they call

the loneliest road in America. Nothing but sun, mountains and desert. Wonderful.'

'You're just an old romantic—just like me. I've been on a couple of camping trips down through France to Spain and I know that feeling first thing in the morning.'

'Two old romantics together,' he said, and for a moment she puzzled over the tone of his voice. But then it changed to something far more brisk.

'Want anything on the radio, on tape? We've even got a couple of CDs for the player.'

'If I'm going to drive in a couple of hours then I think I'll sleep,' she said, 'well, doze anyway.' She was going to be with this man for the next eight or ten hours. Necessarily they'd get to know each other, there'd be half-hidden secrets exchanged, likes and dislikes learned. For now she wanted to take things easy.

But there were three of them in the car. She turned to ask Lucy if there was anything that she wanted to listen to. Lucy pulled off the earphones of her Walkman. 'What?' she asked. So there was no problem there.

Tessa reclined her seat, folded her arms on her lap and shut her eyes. She would see what would happen. And the car purred onwards.

A couple of hours later he pulled in at a service station in Leicester. Lucy was asleep and they didn't stop, just changed places. 'Are you sure you're happy for me to drive?' she asked again.

'If you're as good a driver as you are a nurse then I'm more than happy. Drive for two hours and then we'll change again. Just wake me up.'

'You're going to sleep?' In spite of what he'd said

earlier, she was still a little surprised that he would trust her sufficiently to sleep.

'Why not? It's going to be a long night.'

So she drove. Her own little car was well maintained and powerful enough in its way, but it was nothing like this. This had an automatic gearbox, power-assisted steering and a powerful engine. The car seemed to drive itself. And whereas her own vehicle took its own good time getting up to seventy, this car was there with the lightest touch on the accelerator. She was enjoying herself.

After half an hour there was some kind of problem ahead and all the traffic slowed to a moderate thirty miles an hour. Tessa glanced down at the silent figure by her side. James was asleep—or nearly so. His face looked different. The hard lines had eased and he looked younger. She thought she could see the man he might have been—fourteen years ago? When Lucy was born, when he had lost his wife. She wondered what he would have looked like if that marriage had survived. Would he have looked, acted so hard then? Would he have been a calmer, quieter man? Perhaps so.

There was no sound from Lucy, Tessa glanced over her shoulder. Lucy too was asleep.

She joined the M25. Traffic here was heavier but it still was moving. She drove on.

When they were about to cross the Thames she pulled in at a motorway service area. Even though she drove as gently as possible, James was instantly awake. He sat up and looked out of the window. Then he turned to look at the sleeping Lucy and rearranged the blanket round her.

'My turn to drive. We've been going for over four hours now—how about a drink? Stretch your legs?'

Tessa thought she could detect the tone of a man who was humouring delicate women. 'You stay here with Lucy. I'll fetch a couple of cups of plastic coffee and then we'll be straight on our way. I like to keep going once I've started.'

He looked at her with some interest. 'You knew that's what I wanted, didn't you?' he asked. 'Did you say it to please me?'

'Not at all. It's what I want, too.'

'Good. We seem to agree on quite a few things, don't we? All right, let's have a couple of coffees and then be off.'

When she came back, clutching the two drinks, she saw him leaning against the car with his arms pressed to the roof, doing leg- and back-stretching exercises. He moved gracefully from one exercise to the other. There was the impression of power and tension in his body even when it was still. She knew the exercises, had done them herself. But never had she seen them performed with such determination.

James took over the driving, and they set off on the last stretch of motorway down to the coast. It was dark now but she didn't try to sleep. There was that growing excitement that she always felt when she went abroad.

She'd never been through the Channel tunnel before, and as they queued to be loaded she missed the sight of the ferry looming above her, the shriek of the gulls. But this was exciting, too. Lucy woke, and all three of them had a roll and a drink of juice that Tessa had packed. Then they rumbled up the ramp and onto the carriages that would take them through.

'This is about as exciting as the Mersey Tunnel,' Lucy said after five minutes, 'I'm going back to sleep.' And she did, with the ease of youth.

It was strangely intimate sitting there in the car in the half-darkness, with only the dull rattle of the rails below them. Lucy muttered in her sleep and once again James leaned round to rearrange her blanket. He said nothing.

For the first time on the journey Tessa felt a bit uncomfortable with him—well, not uncomfortable but as if something was missing. There should have been a conversation but she could think of nothing to say.

Perhaps he felt the same way. 'Would you like a tape on?' he asked. 'We could play it quietly, though I doubt if anything could wake Lucy.' He gave her a box to select from. A good idea. Listening to music would stop her feeling odd. She picked out an Elton John tape. 'Yours?' she asked.

'No, that's Lucy's. But I quite like his music.'

Tessa leaned to slip in the tape, tried to put it in the wrong way. He reached for her hand, guided it to the right place. But then he didn't let go at once. Or did he? She couldn't tell—had he squeezed her hand or not? She decided just to listen to the music. At this dark hour of the night you were bound to get odd feelings.

They trundled out of the tunnel, went through a few formalities, and with what seemed like incredible swiftness were on the French autoroute. It was getting light now and the sky had the dreary colour it always held just before sunrise. It was about a hundred miles to Reims and once again she suggested she should drive the middle section. And she tried to doze.

It was the sun on her face that woke her. She

opened her eyes, blinked up at James. He was looking
down at her. 'You smile when you're asleep,' he told
her. 'You seem perfectly contented. I wondered what
dreams you might be having, what made you seem
so happy.'

Tessa thought about her dreams, decided she didn't
want to tell him about them. 'Just looking forward to
today,' she said. 'Nothing special. Why are we stopping?'

He was pulling into a motorway service area—a
fairly quiet one, with the usual trees and landscaping
that made the place look so attractive. 'The sun's up
and we're properly in France now. I'm going to fill
up with petrol and then I thought we might celebrate
by having a real cup of coffee. And if you want you
could go and freshen up.'

'That sounds a great idea.'

She jumped out of the car and took her travelling
bag into the spotless cloakroom. There, she washed
her face, cleaned her teeth and then felt considerably
better. When she came out James was sitting at an
outdoor table, coffee and croissants in front of him.
The still sleeping Lucy was in the car, not far away.

She sat opposite him and reached for her coffee.
'There's something magic about sitting here,' she
said.

'Why magic? Though I do know what you mean.'

She shrugged. 'Oh, the air feels different, the light
isn't the same.'

'And I thought it was being with me.'

'Perhaps it is being with you.' The answer just
slipped out, and she knew at once she shouldn't have
said it. Hastily she added, 'But it's more likely to be

the air and the light and the coffee. Should I wake Lucy?'

He knew what she was doing and smiled. 'No,' he said. 'And I find it magic just being with you.'

Their hotel was modern, a motel really, with a large restaurant attached, situated on the outskirts of the city. They arrived very early and were booked in at once. Tessa had said she would share a room with Lucy—after all, she was meant to be the girl's chaperone. And James had said, yes, perhaps it would be better if the two shared a room.

Lucy managed to tumble out of the car and straight into bed, apparently without waking up. James put down Tessa's case and said, 'I'll go to my room, have a shower and shave and then take a taxi to the conference centre. I probably won't see you both till late tonight. You are going to be all right?'

'Perfectly all right,' said Tessa. 'That's why you brought me, isn't it?' She held up a guide book. 'Lucy and I have plans.'

He handed her some notes. 'I want you to spend this on your day. Take a taxi everywhere, buy whatever the two of you want. Enjoy yourselves.'

She looked at the money. 'We won't need anything like this much!'

'Spend it anyway. You should know how relieved I am to know that Lucy is safe and enjoying herself.' Then he was gone.

Tessa looked at the sleeping Lucy and decided that she could sleep for a couple of hours herself but she would have a shower first. When she'd undressed she stepped into the bathroom and could dimly hear the sounds of a shower from next door. That was James's room. He was having a shower, his naked body not four feet from hers—but separated by a wall. What a thought!

And this thought was still with her as she drifted off to sleep.

'If you tell me that Reims has a fantastic thirteenth-century cathedral, I don't want to know,' said Lucy, over a very late breakfast. 'I don't feel like being a tourist. Aren't these chocolate rolls yummy?'

'Yummy and fattening,' said Tessa. 'We'll have half each of this last one.' She pointed outside. 'The sun's getting up and it's going to be hot. Put on something cool and we'll go to buy you a straw hat. Your dad's given me some money. We'll try the shopping centre, there's quite a good one here.'

Lucy's eyes sparkled. 'That's great! But you've got to buy a hat, too. It's more fun shopping for two.'

It was a good shopping centre, carefully pedestrian-ised. They walked down pleasant flower-bedecked streets, across squares with fountains. In a large store Lucy found the hat she wanted almost straight away but Tessa insisted that they look in at least one more shop. So they checked two more and then returned to the first place. Tessa bought a hat there too.

The two of them stood side by side, admiring their reflections in the full-length mirrors. Tessa's dress was a white cotton, with a silver thread running through. She bought a broad-brimmed straw hat with a white band round it. Lucy's dress was blue so she bought herself a white boater with a black band.

'Don't we look swish,' Lucy said, turning this way and that.

'You look great,' Tessa said. 'Come on, we'll walk along and let a few Frenchmen admire you.'

So they strolled on further, looking in bookshops, clothes shops, shoe shops. Tessa was enjoying herself. This was the kind of morning she had all too rarely.

When they felt vaguely tired Tessa said, 'Time for lunch. Now there's a McDonald's over there or we can go and have something in one of these outdoor cafés.'

'I want to sit on the pavement like all these others. That way we can look at people passing by and make comments on them.'

'Sounds like a good idea.'

So they sat on the pavement under a striped umbrella, had more coffee and ordered a *croque monsieur*—which turned out to be a toasted ham and cheese sandwich.

They sat there for a further half-hour and had another coffee. It was fun, sitting there in the warmth, chatting idly, saying nothing very much.

'I've never quite done this before. I suppose this is the sort of afternoon you have with a mother,' Lucy said after a while, and Tessa tensed. It had just been a casual remark, but she could see all sorts of trouble ahead.

'What do you mean?' she asked, trying to be equally casual.

Lucy shrugged. 'Buying clothes, talking about them. My friends at my old school were always going out with their mothers to buy stuff.'

'Well…what do you do?'

'I go shopping with Dad. We get the clothes all right but shopping with him is no fun. I suggest something and he decides if it's suitable. But he doesn't actually enjoy shopping with me. It's not something he'd choose to do.'

'I would have thought he loved being out with you.'

'I think he does, but he doesn't enjoy shopping. For him it's just a means to an end. To enjoy shopping you need a mother. And I haven't got one.'

This time there was a definite sense of loss in her words. It was an invitation to talk, and Tessa wondered if she should take it. She decided she would, but she'd be cautious.

'Your dad didn't tell me about your mother,' she said, 'so perhaps it's not a good idea if you do.'

'She's my mother, I can talk about her if I want!' Lucy showed a touch of temper, which she hadn't done for a while. 'He told me about her just a couple of years ago. When, as he said, I was turning into a young lady and had the right to know. He told me about how they parted, how it could be thought nobody's fault. He leaned over backwards to be fair to her. He said he'd give me her address and I could write to her if I wanted to. It was entirely up to me— so he said—but I could tell from his face what he wanted me to do. So I did that. I didn't write.'

'Did you really want to write?'

Lucy didn't answer at first. Tessa waited patiently. She felt very sorry for Lucy. She's only fourteen, Tessa thought, even if she's got the body and the presence of a much older girl. She's lost, she's trying to cope with more than a fourteen-year-old should have to cope with.

'No, I didn't want to write,' Lucy said eventually. 'Dad can be as hard as nails sometimes but I know he cares for me and I wouldn't consciously do anything to hurt him.'

'Like run away to London?'

'That,' Lucy said with a blush, 'was a gesture.' She went on, 'I didn't want to write but I would have liked a mum. But it looks like I can't have both.' She drained her coffee. 'Come on,' she said, 'we'd better visit this cathedral. If we don't, my new French teacher will never forgive me.'

So they visited the cathedral and both were enthralled.

'So, did you have a good day?' James asked.

They were back in their hotel room. Lucy was in her pyjamas, sitting on the bed, trying to make sense of French television. Both she and Tessa had enjoyed their day, but the travel the night before had tired them, so they'd taken a taxi back, had a quick meal in the restaurant downstairs and Lucy at least was now ready for bed.

'Had a great day, Dad.' She grinned. 'Tessa and me went mad, shopping. How was your day?'

'Tiring but very useful. I got a couple of very good ideas on—'

Lucy yawned loudly. 'Boring, boring,' she said. 'I need to go to sleep. I know Tessa isn't tired yet because she's a medical person and everybody knows that they don't need sleep, so why don't you take her down to the bar for half an hour?'

Tessa had been listening to this exchange, thinking how well the two of them could get on. James turned to her. 'You won't find a conversation about new resuscitation techniques boring, will you?' he asked. 'I should have asked before—did you enjoy your day and would you like a drink? I could certainly do with one myself.'

'Yes, I'd like a drink,' Tessa said, 'but give me five minutes to change, will you?'

'Make it ten minutes and I'll shower and change as well.' He came over, bent to kiss his daughter. Lucy threw her arms round his neck. ''Night, sweetheart. I'm glad you had a good day, you can tell me about it tomorrow.' He glanced at his watch. 'Down at the bar in ten minutes, Tessa?' Then he left.

'Wear that longish blue dress I saw you hang up,' Lucy suggested. 'That'll show him that you're not just a chaperone. He must think you're some kind of Mary Poppins.'

Tessa took out the dress and held it against herself. She had brought it but now she was wondering about wearing it. It had a lowish front and the skirt was split to mid-thigh. It made her look…well, un-nursish and not in the least like Mary Poppins. 'All right, I'll wear it,' she said, 'and I think I'll do something with my hair.'

In the bar were waiters in starched shirts, dim lighting, very comfortable leather seats. She and Lucy had peeped into it earlier but decided not to go inside.

James was waiting for her by the entrance to save her the embarrassment of walking in alone. That was thoughtful of him, Tessa thought. Before he had been wearing his consultant 'uniform'—the dark suit, white shirt, college tie. Now he was in a much lighter linen suit, with an open-necked shirt. Casual, she thought, but still very smart.

He led her to a seat and sat beside her. A hovering waiter promptly took their orders for two red wines and put a small tray of nuts in front of them. James looked at her and smiled. 'You don't know how much it meant to me, knowing that Lucy was safe and happy,' he said. 'That really made my day.'

'Are you sure she was happy?' Tessa asked.

'If not, she'd have let me know somehow. And if you couldn't give her a good time, then no one could.'

Tessa liked the compliment. 'Both of us had a good time,' she said. 'Lucy is good company. Now, tell me about these new techniques in resuscitation.'

'You know about the golden hour—that time immediately after an accident when so many lives are either saved or lost—well, how would it be if…?'

She listened attentively. What he said made a great deal of sense. If introduced, the techniques would undeniably save lives. But a lot of changes would have to be made.

'It sounds really good.' She nodded. 'But where's the money to come from?'

'I'll get it out of the hospital somehow. We owe it to our patients.'

When he spoke like that she felt a little sorry for the hospital administrators. Arguing with James would not be easy. If he thought he was right—don't stand in his way. She admired his resolution, his determination to change things for the better.

'Our last consultant didn't feel the same way about things,' she said. 'He thought the department was running pretty well as it was.'

'That man was a waste of space and should have been sacked years ago,' James said flatly.

Tessa was a little surprised at James saying that, though there was a lot of truth in it. 'Hey, what about professional courtesy?' she asked impishly.

'It should never get in the way of the well-being of patients or, for that matter, the morale of the staff!

That man just ambled along and...' Then he realised she was teasing him. 'You're making fun of me,' he said, 'a poor tired consultant who only wants what's best for his patients.'

'Me? Make fun of someone as important as you? Never! But I do think you ought to relax more.'

'Relax more?' He pondered. 'Well, Tessa, teach me how to relax more. Do you want me to lie on the floor and think soothing thoughts when I get mad?'

'Why not? I do it sometimes and it works for me. I've got a sheepskin rug in my sitting room and that does just fine.'

His eyes gleamed. 'The very idea of you lying on the floor on a sheepskin rug produces thoughts in me that are definitely not soothing.'

Tessa felt herself getting rather red. She had better get this conversation back on track. 'Have you always been driven? Always determined to get on no matter what stands in your way?'

He considered this. 'I think so. Certainly I was that way after my wife left. I decided on two things. First, I would get on in medicine. Second, Lucy would never suffer from not having a mother.'

'You've done very well on both counts.'

He grinned. 'Perhaps so. Though I think that recently I've been falling behind a little with Lucy. There are areas which a father just can't enter.'

Delicately, Tessa asked, 'Have you ever considered—if only for Lucy's sake—getting married again?'

'You don't mind living dangerously, do you? Ask anything if it leads to the truth?'

'I don't want to pry. But I think it's a fair question.'

'Perhaps so.' For a moment she wished she hadn't

asked. James was obviously tired and working out a careful answer was tiring him even more. But she did want to know. Eventually he said, 'I still have this tremendous feeling that marriage should be for ever. Perhaps I was the cause of the failure before, I wouldn't want to make another woman unhappy. I have had a couple of half-hearted affairs that seemed to drift into nothing. Probably because I was unwilling—or reluctant—to commit myself. Why am I telling you all this?'

He really seemed to want an answer to his question. So Tessa said, 'Because you bottle too much up and it's good to let things out. Because you're tired and in a foreign country. Because you know I'll never say anything—though I might talk about people like you on one of my programmes.'

'Fame at last,' he muttered. 'Tessa, you've missed one reason why I find it easy to confide in you. It's because you're a very attractive woman.'

Once again she had the feeling of slipping into waters that were too deep for her. 'Thank you. But remember—these three days we're keeping things strictly professional.'

'Probably the best thing.'

She wondered if he was disappointed. Certainly she was. Still, she'd better think of something else to talk about. 'Lucy is fourteen. In seven years she'll be twenty-one. She'll be starting her own career, there will be young men in her life, she'll have to make her own decisions. How are you going to cope with that?'

'Badly, I suspect,' he said mournfully, and both of them laughed.

'She'll want a man just like you,' Tessa predicted.

'One day you'll open the door and there'll be you, only twenty-two years younger.'

'Heaven help us all,' he said. 'Do you know, you've just ruined my evening. I think I'd hate a younger me.'

Tessa was really enjoying herself, but she couldn't help it. She yawned.

'And there's a hint,' he said cheerfully. 'Perhaps we'd better both get off to our beds. You must be as tired as I am.'

'That might be a good idea,' she admitted. But she didn't think it was a good idea because she was tired. It was a good idea because she didn't quite know where the evening was going. She was learning more and more about James and she was getting dangerously fond of his company.

He walked her to her room. She paused there, key in hand, and looked up at him almost fearfully. He took her by the shoulders, bent to kiss her cheek. He hesitated, then he kissed her on the lips. Tessa could have stopped him, but it was only a gentle goodnight kiss. Then slowly his hold on her tightened, and she found herself melting into his arms.

Suddenly things had changed. The reason for their trip was forgotten, the presence of his sleeping daughter behind the door was forgotten. His kiss was now that of a lover. She felt her lips part, felt the sweet intrusion of his tongue and knew she needed much more. Wherever he was touching her, her body tensed. She thought that she knew him as surely as if they had both been naked. Kiss her much more and she would... He released her.

Tessa looked up at him, knowing that hurt and surprise were showing in her face. And James looked equally shocked. She thought the kiss had bewildered them both. What had started as a small courtesy had turned into something much deeper. She was unnerved at the feelings pulsing through her.

'Goodnight, James.' Frantically she scrabbled with her key, managed to open the door without looking at him again.

'Goodnight, Tessa.'

She crept into her darkened bedroom, through to the bathroom and then into bed. She closed her eyes but she knew she wouldn't sleep. There were two problems here. First was her physical reaction to James—her body had betrayed her. But she could live with this. After all she was a young healthy woman. There was something worse. She longed for James in a way that was much deeper than simple bodily attraction.

It was still sunny the next day. In the morning Tessa and Lucy went on a trip James had organised for them, touring the region where they grew the grapes for making champagne and finishing at one of the great houses where they made the sparkling wine. Both Tessa and Lucy found it surprisingly interesting and enjoyed the complimentary glass of wine. In the afternoon they went back to the centre of Reims and shopped.

They had intended to go back to the hotel and have a meal there as they had done the night before. But when they arrived, James was waiting for them.

'Dad! We didn't expect you for hours yet.'

'I decided to sneak off early. There was nothing much left that I was interested in, so I thought I would ask the two women in my life if they'd like to come out to dinner with me. Tessa?'

'That would be lovely,' Tessa said. And she saw how pleased Lucy was.

They took a taxi to a restaurant that had been recommended in a little village not too far away. They ate outside, under a veranda hung with grapevines. Afterwards Tessa remembered that the meal had been fantastic—but she couldn't remember a single thing she'd eaten. It was just so good to be part of this little family.

Next day they drove home. Once again Tessa shared the driving. They'd set off early in the morning and expected to be home by late evening. Lucy again managed to sleep most of the way.

As they were driven through the Channel tunnel, Tessa said, 'I usually think that the trip back is a bit depressing. Holidays are over, it's time to get back to work. But although I've enjoyed myself this time, I don't feel that way.'

'Me neither. I've got the feeling that I'm going back to something new, something starting. But what?'

'Reorganising the department?' she asked.

'You know better than that,' he said.

· CHAPTER SIX

THE next day Tessa called round at the radio station for a quick word with Ray after she'd finished work. He listened carefully to what she had to say.

'Certainly June is short-handed,' he said. 'I'm surprised she copes with the amount of work she has. But this is a shoestring operation. We don't have much money and it's always bad to mix business and kindness.'

'She wouldn't need much money,' Tessa said. 'She could just work in the back room, filing stuff, and have the baby in there with her. I was thinking perhaps three hours every morning?'

'See what June says. If she's agreeable then we'll give it a week's trial.'

June was doubtful, but she was overworked and was willing to see how things went. So Tessa drove round to Anita Barnes's flat. 'How do you fancy a part-time job?' she asked.

It was a day for making decisions. While she was working, later that afternoon, James came and asked to speak to her. He spoke to her in an oddly formal manner. 'Tessa, Lucy wondered if you'd be free to come to dinner on Saturday evening?'

'Lucy wondered?'

'Well, I should have said Lucy and myself. But perhaps you've got plans for Saturday night. An at-

tractive young woman like you must…well, there
must be plenty of…'

'I've got no plans for Saturday evening,' she told
him, 'and I'd love to come to dinner. But won't people talk? A staff nurse going to dinner with her consultant?'

'It's possible. But I think you'll be seen as coming
as Lucy's guest, not mine. Shall we say eight o'clock,
then?'

'I'm looking forward to it.'

When he'd gone she shook her head in vexation.
What was wrong with the man? He talked as if their
three days in France had never happened.

Tessa arrived early at the radio station for her Friday
night talk. Ray had phoned, saying he had some news
for her.

'These things take time,' he said. 'There'll be committee meetings and decisions to be vetted and so on.
But I've heard unofficially that you went down very
well last Saturday. All three of them thought that you
handled the interview really well. But, more important, they liked your voice. It's like I've always said—
it's a natural radio voice. People hear it and think
you're their friend. You could be going places,
Tessa.'

She supposed this was good news, but at the moment she wasn't in the mood for talking about a different future. 'I don't know, Ray. There's a lot happening in my life at the moment. I don't know if I
can handle any more change.'

Ray looked at her closely, decided not to question
her. 'Just don't take any quick decisions,' he told her,

'and remember, this is a great new chance. Now, what have you got for tonight?'

She passed over her script, and as he read it she thought about what was really new in her life. The only new thing was Lucy or, to be honest, James. How were they going to affect her?

'Lots of people get hurt when relationships fall apart, Barry. It's a risk you just have to take. If you offer some of yourself then you're vulnerable. But just because you've been hurt it doesn't mean that you shouldn't try again. Remember the best parts of what you had before. Perhaps you can have those again. It's too easy to retreat into yourself, to say that this kind of happiness isn't for you. Take a chance! You might be happily surprised.'

'You were good, like you always are,' said Ray in the pub afterwards. 'What I want to know is, are you going to take your own advice? Are you going to take a chance?'

'I guess I am,' Tessa said slowly. But she was still not sure what she had agreed to.

A Saturday night dinner with James and Lucy. From the formal way she had been invited, it was obvious that it was to be a formal dinner. So what should she wear? She seemed to have been more bothered about clothes in the last couple of weeks than she had in the past five years.

The weather was still warm so she would have to dress accordingly. Eventually she decided on a sleeveless top and a long linen skirt. She could carry a wrap in case it got cold later.

She decided to take a taxi, which would mean she

could drink more than her usual one glass of wine. James would certainly offer her wine and she wanted to enjoy it.

When she thought about it she realised that she had never been to dinner with a man before. Not in his home, with him as the host. She would have taken a hostess flowers or chocolates—what did you take as a gift for a man? Wine was out—he knew far more about it than she did. Eventually she decided that flowers would be all right and bought a sheaf of roses. Then she added to that idea, and from a craft shop she knew she bought him a hand-thrown pot. The combination of red and white flowers looked good in the earthenware pot.

Why was she worrying so much? This was only a courtesy visit because she had helped him with Lucy. Wasn't it?

She was still apprehensive when she arrived at the front door. 'Tessa, it's so good to see you!' She was greeted by both James and Lucy, which she thought rather nice. Like her, Lucy was dressed in a long skirt, but instead of having her hair flowing had put it up in a very smart style. James was in his lightweight suit again. She remembered him wearing it during their conversation in the bar in Reims—only five nights ago?

Both seemed very pleased to see her. She thought how lovely it was when they smiled—unlike the scowling faces she'd seen when she'd first met them both.

'I've bought you a pot,' she said, offering it to him, 'and some flowers to put in it. I thought you might like it on your desk. Of course, if you don't...' She realised she was mumbling, and stopped.

'Oh, I do want it on my desk. Sometimes I think my room needs a woman's touch, and this will provide it.'

'I can't do the woman's touch yet,' Lucy said with a grin. 'I'm only a girl. Now I've got to amuse and entertain you while Dad finishes in the kitchen.'

'Dad finishes in the kitchen?'

'I do all the cooking in this house. I'm an expert.'

'Oh! Would you like me to help you? I could—'

'Certainly not! I don't allow interlopers in my kitchen.'

'I'll play for you if you like,' Lucy said, 'just for a minute or two.'

'I'd like that very much.' Tessa felt she needed time to think, to ready herself for what might come. She suspected that this evening was going to be, well, eventful.

James served dinner in the conservatory at the back of the house. It was pleasant because doors were open on both sides. The cooling breeze that blew through and the plants in the conservatory made Tessa feel as if she were dining out of doors.

The meal was exquisite. Cold watercress soup with hot rolls, salmon and salad, an ice cream that was obviously home-made. The white wine he served she guessed was very different from the five-pound bottles she usually bought.

'This is wonderful, James.' She smiled. 'You did it all yourself? No one came in to help or brought things?'

He looked aggrieved. 'Certainly not! I taught myself to cook when Lucy was a child. I didn't want her to grow up eating beans and fish fingers.'

'But I didn't like his fancy food,' Lucy said, grinning again. 'I wanted beans and fish fingers.'

'Cooking is only chemistry,' James said, 'and I used to be a good chemist.'

'It's more than that to you,' Tessa said. 'I can tell by the way you talk about cooking. You love it.'

'Yes, well, perhaps so. I find cooking for someone you…like a lot is very satisfying.'

'Then Lucy's been very lucky,' Tessa said carefully.

'Well, I've spent as much time with her as I could. Haven't I, sweetheart?'

'You've been a good dad, by and large,' Lucy allowed. 'Well, not a bad one. Tessa, sorry to say this, especially since I so much wanted you to come, but I've got to go out. There's a rehearsal for a youth concert I'm taking part in and they've just brought it forward.'

'That's fine,' said Tessa. 'We can have a chat another time.' But then she wondered how would she cope with an evening alone with James. Could he have arranged this? She decided not—that wasn't James's style.

'You'd better go and change,' James said. 'Your taxi'll be here in ten minutes.'

'Right.' Lucy hesitated, obviously wondering how to say something. Tessa glanced from daughter to father. What next?

'There's a little group going for coffee after the rehearsal. I know they're a bit older than me but I've been invited, and I'd like to go, too.'

Tessa saw James hesitate. His eyes flicked towards her. Then he said, 'You're getting to be grown-up. I've every confidence that you'll act responsibly. I know Tessa thinks that I should give you a freer rein—so off you go.'

'Daddy!' Lucy kissed him, rushed out.

So now she was to spend the entire evening alone with James. How did she feel about that? Half excited, half apprehensive, she thought. Tessa looked at him, and had the uneasy feeling that he knew exactly what she'd been thinking.

'Now Lucy has gone we can have another glass of wine. Would you like to come out into the garden?' He led her to a little arbour where two easy chairs faced each other.

She sipped her wine and said, 'You let Lucy stay on after the rehearsal. I'm not entirely sure about you involving me in that decision. I know it was my advice but...now I feel that I'm responsible.'

'If you give advice, you must be responsible. Anyway, I'm glad to shed some of the blame. Have you any idea what it cost me to say what I did?'

She thought. 'I can imagine. I know you've got a reputation for driving your staff, making sure they work right up to their limit. But then you'll support them, too.'

'You've been checking up on me? Getting stories from my old hospital?' He seemed mildly amused.

'Of course. You know, medicine is a small world. But children aren't like members of staff. Often they can't be driven, they have to be led.'

'You're telling me. I think I know that now.'

Discreetly she asked, 'Have you had no help in bringing up Lucy? Didn't her mother want to...? Wasn't she interested...?'

He smiled. 'You want to know about my ex-wife. I suppose that's understandable. But there are some things I want to keep to myself. I don't want the hospital knowing everything about me.'

Deliberately she finished her wine, set the glass down on the table in front of her. She stood. 'I think I'll go now. I have as much regard for confidentiality as any doctor, and it's insulting to me to suggest otherwise. Thank you for a very enjoyable meal, James.'

As she turned he leapt to his feet, reached out to her. Then he lowered his arm. 'Tessa, please! Stop a minute!'

'Why? So you can insult me some more?'

She could tell by his face that he wasn't angry—there was none of the black-faced scowling that she knew so well. If anything, he looked upset. Eventually he said formally, 'I am sorry. I offended you and I apologise. I spoke without thinking and I hurt you unnecessarily. Now...Tessa, will you please sit down again and let me pour you another glass of wine?'

She hesitated. In many ways this would be a good chance for her to leave. She didn't know what might happen if she stayed. She had a feeling that she was teetering on the edge of an abyss—if she fell, there would be nothing she could do to help herself. But, really, she knew she wanted to fall.

She sat down and silently held out her glass for him to refill. 'I don't know much about wine but I can tell this is good.'

'A Sancerre. I must save a glass for Lucy.'

That intrigued Tessa. 'You encourage her to drink wine?'

'She's had an occasional glass of wine, with water usually, regularly since her eleventh birthday. I thought that if she grew up seeing it as one of life's ordinary pleasures, she would be more likely to drink in moderation as an adult.'

'That's very…thoughtful of you.'

'You mean, not what you would have thought of me?'

She laughed. 'Sorry. I'm afraid you're right.'

Then they seemed to be more at ease with each other. Tessa found she was enjoying herself. It was pleasant to sit here in the warmth, in a comfortable chair, with the sounds and scents of summer around her. And the company of an intriguing man.

'Tessa I'd like to tell you about Michelle—Lucy's mother.' James's voice was soft, reflective. 'I brought Lucy up myself. I've done the very best I could, though it hasn't been easy. Especially since I was trying to pursue a career at the same time.' He laughed. 'There's been plenty of good advice, but most of it was contradictory.'

'You had no family to help you?' Tessa asked.

'None. I tried assorted nannies and so on. Some were good and some were less so. The two best of them got married and had to follow their husbands. But Lucy was always my responsibility.'

'A child should be more than a responsibility,' Tessa said gently. 'She should be a joy.'

'Oh, she was that, too. Well, until she was twelve. Then she became a monster. Adolescence! I'm sure I wasn't a pain like Lucy.'

'I'm sure you were. And don't worry about adolescence—it'll last until she's thirty.'

They both laughed again, and Tessa felt a warm bond of comfort with him. They were getting on so well. She had always felt that he was a caring father, but listening to him talk proved it to her.

'Lucy seems a very gifted musician,' she went on. 'Does she get it from you?'

'She is very gifted. I've tried to encourage her but not too much—I want her to be sure it's what she really wants. So far she's been sensible. I'm pleased with that.'

He paused for a moment and when he spoke again his voice was flatter. 'She doesn't get it from me, though,' he said. 'She gets it from her mother.'

The pause this time was much longer. 'You're either going to tell me or you're not,' said Tessa. 'You'd better make up your mind.'

He shook his head. 'In many ways you're a very remarkable woman, Tessa. You don't believe in taking prisoners.'

He poured them both yet another glass of wine. Tessa knew that he was preparing himself and he needed time to get his thoughts in order. For the first time she saw this man, who had always been so certain of things, wonder if he was right. And this small show of sudden vulnerability made him seem even more attractive.

'I know some people think I'm hard—certainly in some ways. Well, perhaps I am, but that's better than being in a perpetual fog of uncertainty.' He frowned. 'I believe that marriages should last. It's too easy to get married, too easy to break up and separate. And when children are involved, marriages should be for ever.'

Now came that black look again. 'I met Michelle Trenet when I was a twenty-year-old medical student in London. She was older than me, very beautiful. I was impressed that she should choose me. Like me, she was a career person—though she was a famous violinist.'

'I think I've heard of her,' Tessa said. 'She's quite famous. Does concerts and so on.'

'She is quite famous. But she'd say not famous enough. Anyway, we lived together on and off. She got pregnant, we got married. It wasn't a good idea, but I was ready to do the best I could. I wanted to make it work. We had Lucy. Michelle wasn't an ideal mother, though I suppose I wasn't an ideal husband. I thought she should have put her career on hold until I qualified—certainly while Lucy was very young.'

Tessa could see what this account was costing him. He was trying to be fair, to be objective. But there was a bitterness underneath that kept breaking through.

'Six months after Lucy was born Michelle was offered a job—a concert tour in America. It was make or break for her, she said, she had to go. But she couldn't take the baby. I won't tell you about the arguments, the concessions, the stand-up rows that we had. She went on the tour. I looked after Lucy. After another three months she wrote, saying the marriage had been a mistake and she didn't want motherhood to ruin her career. She wanted a divorce, so I gave her a divorce. And I got custody of Lucy.'

'Did she fight it?' Tessa asked after another pause.

'No. She was more than happy. And at the end of the day, I think it all happened for the best.'

Tessa thought about this story. 'Did you feel trapped?' she asked. 'It must have been awfully hard, bringing up a child on your own. And studying medicine.'

He thought. 'Yes, I felt a bit trapped. But mostly I felt blessed.'

Tessa thought that was a lovely thing to say. She felt sorry for him and yet she admired him. Delicately, she asked, 'Has there been no woman in your life since?' Then she added hurriedly, 'I meant as a mother to Lucy.'

He grinned. 'Of course you did. No, but there has never been anyone who I would have wanted as the mother of my child.'

'Well, as a single father, I think you've done incredibly well.'

'Thank you. That's a compliment I appreciate. Now...fair is fair. Will you tell me about you?'

'Me? What about me?'

'You're a very attractive young woman, bright as well as beautiful. There should be a long line of men waiting to take you out, but you seem to actively discourage them. Once again, this isn't a compliment, it's an observation. So will you tell me about yourself?'

It was a fair question and she knew she had to answer him. But now she was feeling the anxiety she realised James had felt—the fear of revealing too much. 'Well, there is a story,' she started, 'but it's a bit—'

His mobile phone rang. He listened for a moment, then motioned for Tessa to put her head close to his so she could hear, too. It was Lucy.

'Dad? When I've finished the rehearsal and after the coffee-bar, I've been invited to this boy's house for supper. He plays the piano, like me. He's called David Cross. He says his mother will speak to you if you like.'

James looked at Tessa, raising his eyebrows. She nodded.

'That'll be fine, sweetheart. You go and enjoy yourself. It doesn't matter about his mother phoning, though she can if she wants. You still come back by taxi. Keep your mobile switched on in case I need to contact you—OK?'

'Fine. I love you, Dad! Bye!'

James looked at Tessa again. 'Lucy's growing up. Or perhaps I am.'

'Sometimes I think that we don't ever finish growing up.'

He sighed. 'The trouble with you, Tessa, is that you're so often and so obviously right. Now, are you going to tell me about yourself?'

He had a right to know. He had revealed aspects of himself that she suspected few people had ever seen, and it was only fair that she do the same. But not now.

'There is a story and I promise to tell you, but can we wait a while? It always makes me feel so bad and I…I really am enjoying myself.'

'Of course,' he said gently, 'but, remember, I do want to know.' His voice altered. 'Now, we've nearly finished the wine and it's getting dark. How about coming inside and having coffee?'

'Yes, I'd like that.' So they had coffee, with thin, dark chocolate biscuits, and talked generally about medical matters. In some ways it had been an emotionally fraught evening and they both needed to be calm for a while. And then she knew it was a good time for her to go.

'I'll come in the taxi with you,' he offered.

'No, you'd better stay here and wait for your

daughter. She'll want to tell you how things have been, she needs to have you here.'

'Very well.' James phoned for a taxi from the firm that she always used. And as they waited in the hall he took her in his arms and kissed her. She'd known he would. This was a gentle, loving kiss, unlike that kiss of unexpected passion in France. She put her arms round him and pulled him closer.

After a while he took his lips from hers, but they stayed together with their arms loosely round each other. 'I haven't been kissed like that for a long time,' she said dreamily. 'It was so nice. I liked it and you made me feel...safe.'

'Safe?' There was an element of dry humour in his voice. 'Shouldn't a lover be passionate—dangerous rather than safe?'

'I've had passion and danger. Now I need to feel safe. But there's still a bit of me that says I should run a mile from you.'

'But is there another bit that says something else? That you should stay, not run?'

'Oh, yes. I'm feeling...feelings that I haven't allowed myself in years.'

'So am I. Do you think we have any kind of future together?'

She hesitated. 'It would be nice to think so. We're standing here in the half-dark, kissing like two teenagers, and I'm remembering when life seemed a lot simpler than it is.'

'I know. I think there's a bit of my life that has been left out—dating, it's called. What do you do on a date? I'm not sure any more how to ask a girl if I can take her out.'

She giggled. 'First of all we look at our respective

diaries, find what is called "a window of opportunity". Then we decide what we want to do.'

'Sounds a bit cold-blooded, but I suppose you're right. Tessa, may I climb through your window of opportunity?'

'That sounds a bit forward but yes. James, you know I'm a bit frightened of this.'

'I've had mad passion before and look where it got me. I think we should both be cautious.' His voice changed in tone. 'Lord, Tessa that must rank as the most timid declaration of love there has ever been!'

'Love?' she asked.

'I guess the word slipped out,' he muttered.

'So what do you want to do?'

He considered. 'I think days are better for getting to know people than nights. Going to France didn't count, I was always aware that Lucy was there. Can we go out together soon? We'll consult our diaries and see if there's one of these windows this week.'

'That would be nice. Now, do you want to kiss me again?'

He did. But this time the gentleness quickly disappeared. His body was pressed to hers, she could feel the urgency in him, the need for her. Her lips parted, she couldn't hold out against the determination of his kiss. And she didn't want to! Now she knew that being together here with him was what she had always wanted. She was his. Whatever he wanted he could have, she couldn't resist him. No, she didn't want to resist him. She could feel her body coming alive, her lips, breasts, thighs electrified by his presence. Lucy was out, perhaps they could...

Dimly, she heard something. He heard it, too, and

reluctantly his grip on her loosened. Outside was a
taxi which hooted softly. She had to ease him away.

'We've started something that must be finished,'
he whispered softly.

'I know.' It was the only answer she could give.

CHAPTER SEVEN

TESSA was on lates for the next week and she only saw James in the distance. Perhaps that was a good thing as she needed to think about what had happened. It was entirely out of character for her. She decided she would wait and see what happened. She was both afraid and hopeful—an odd combination. Whatever, she knew her life was going to change.

It was towards the end of her Thursday shift. Things hadn't been too busy and she was looking forward to going home. But then, when she had twenty minutes to go, four drunks came into the department. One had fallen and cut his arm quite badly, but was too drunk to feel the pain.

The triage nurse decided the best thing was to treat the injured man quickly and get him out of the building. She chose Tessa as the most experienced nurse to do it.

The job wasn't difficult. The cut was really quite minor and had to be cleaned and then stitched. The man hadn't lost enough blood to require a transfusion.

It wasn't an unusual situation. The man kept on shutting his eyes and then reaching out, apparently accidentally, to touch her chest. Tessa sharply told him twice to stop it. 'I might hurt you!' she warned.

'Oh, Nurse! And you an angel of mercy!'

Tessa brushed his hand aside and tried to carry on with her work.

'How's it going, Terry? See you're doing all right

112

for yourself. Nurse, will you see to me when you've
finished with my mate?'

Tessa turned and sighed. The three drunken friends
had turned up, though they should have stayed in
Reception. 'I can't work with you here,' she said.
'Please, leave. Now!'

'Oh, Nurse! You want to be alone with him. She
wants to undress you, Terry!'

Tessa noticed that one of the three was drinking
from a flat bottle he'd taken from his pocket. That
was all she needed. However, she had to try. 'I've
got a job to do here and you're not making it any
easier.'

'You can do a job on me any time—'

'You! You're not allowed drink in this department
and you're not allowed back here anyway. Put that
bottle away and get out!'

James! Where had he come from? She hadn't
known he was in the department.

The man with the bottle looked at James and deliberately took a drink. Then he offered the bottle to
his mate. Somehow the bottle disappeared from his
hand—and James was pouring the contents down the
nearest sink.

'Here! What do you think you're—' One of the
drunks stepped forward—and then stepped backwards
as James walked forward himself. Tessa glanced at
James, and guessed why the lout had backed off. She
had never seen such fury on a face.

'The three of you, get out. Out of the cubicle, out
of this department, out of this hospital. In five minutes
Security will be here. They'll hand you over to the
police and that'll mean a night in the cells. Now,
don't argue, move!'

Tessa wondered if he would get away with it. The three hesitated and the apparent ringleader said, 'We only wanted—'

'Who asked you to speak? I told you to move!'

There was another tense moment. Tessa looked from the three drunks to James. And then the drunks moved out. She breathed a sigh of relief. It was over.

But James hadn't finished yet. He leaned over the now silent figure on the trolley. 'You! This nurse is trying to help you. Keep your hands to yourself or I'll come here and stitch them together. And that's a promise!' He opened the curtain of the cubicles and then said, 'Everything all right now, Nurse Calvert?'

'Everything is fine, Mr Armstrong, thank you. I can cope.' The curtain dropped back in position.

Tessa bent over to carry on with her suturing. 'Who was that?' the now cowed man asked.

'A doctor who has been up for the past eighteen hours, looking after people like you. Now, get straight home and rest. Don't have any more alcohol, it could send you into shock. You don't need to come back here, your GP can take out these stitches in a day or two.'

Terry rose from the trolley and scurried away, and Tessa went looking for James. She was angry.

'James, there was no need for strong-arm tactics just then. I could have coped with the situation. It's something that nurses have to deal with in A and E. Thanks for your help, but it wasn't necessary.'

'I see no reason why nurses in my department should have to cope with that kind of thing. And when I see it, I'll stop it.'

'Well, thanks. But I don't think much of your policy of aggression. What if that man with the bottle hadn't backed down? You could have been badly hurt.'

He shrugged. 'It's been my experience that when you back out of a fight, things get worse. There comes a point when you take no more—no matter what the cost. And if I'd been hurt myself, I'd have asked you to patch me up. You're a very good nurse.' He smiled, and suddenly Tessa discovered that she wasn't angry any more.

'I've handled troublemakers in the past.'

'I'm sure you have. You're expert, experienced. But what if it had been one of our younger nurses? Sally Kent or someone like that? It would upset them badly.' He frowned. 'I remember once when I was very young and working in A and E on a Saturday night. A similar situation to this, a fighting mad drunk brought in. I examined the man. He wasn't seriously hurt, just abrasions and contusions. I told the nurse to clean him up and send him on his way. We were very busy, I had cases piling up. I did think of staying as he wasn't a pleasant man but I thought he'd at least realise that she was trying to help him.'

'And?' Tessa prompted when he didn't continue.

'He lashed out and broke her jaw. She left nursing after that.'

'And in spite of everything that people told you, that it wasn't your fault, that these things happen, that you acted perfectly correctly—you felt guilty?'

'I still do,' he said.

'"There comes a point when you take no more— no matter what the cost,"' she quoted. 'I'll think about that.'

They gazed at each other. 'To jump from the professional to the personal,' he said, 'I see from the

roster that you've got this Saturday off. So have I.
May I take you out somewhere? I thought we could
go out into the country.' He grinned. 'I'm asking you
for a date, Tessa.'

'It sounds lovely. Shall I wear my walking boots
and so on?'

'Not this time. It's supposed to be good weather so
wear whatever you like. We'll be on grass, though,
so don't wear high heels.'

She was enchanted. 'Where are we going?'

He smiled engagingly. 'I want it to be a surprise.'

Next morning she found herself thinking about what
James had said while she was looking through her
mail. Many of her answers involved referring people
on to other authorities. She had a great store of pam-
phlets, addresses where people could get help, but she
always liked to add at least a small personal message.

Then there were the letters in which the answer to
the problem was obvious. Quite often she suspected
the writer knew what he or she had to do. They only
wanted confirmation, some kind of authority for an
action. If they knew that someone was genuinely concerned it was often a great comfort.

And then there were the letters where she had to
think about long and hard before answering. She was
dealing with people's lives, it was a responsibility.
She had one such letter in front of her, but the problem was heart-breakingly common. The woman had
two young children. When her husband drank he
came home and usually beat her—and sometimes the
children. But when he sobered up he was sorry, asked
for forgiveness and said it would never happen again.

Tessa decided to make this letter the basis of her

talk. She would talk about the options—counselling, Alcoholics Anonymous and so on. But she would take as her theme what James had said. 'There comes a point where you take no more—no matter what the cost.' Sometimes it was necessary not to suffer further. She might even hint at what had happened in the A and E department. It would be a good subject, she decided.

Ray said the script was great. She made the broadcast and, yes, she was pleased with it. Ray said there would be plenty of letters commenting on it—always a good thing.

Ray had come across to the Black Lion for the usual drink but then had to leave quite early. Now Tessa was sitting with Anita Barnes. Anita had managed to get a babysitter for the evening and had been delighted to come out for a drink with Tessa and Ray. Tessa suspected that was the first time in quite a while that Anita had been able to get out for a drink with friends and she was obviously enjoying it.

They had just got another drink each when Tessa's mobile phone rang. 'I listened to your talk tonight, it was good. I noticed you quoted me and I was rather pleased.'

'Yes, well,' she said, 'I'm not saying that I agree with everything you say, but perhaps your views have affected me.'

'Strange. I would have said the opposite. I think you have affected me more.'

Her views had affected James? There was a thought.

'Looking forward to seeing you tomorrow,' he said. 'Lucy's gone to bed early with a bit of a headache, I think she's been overdoing things. So I think I'll have an early night, too. Goodnight, Tessa.'

'Goodnight James.' He had rung her at once to tell her he thought her broadcast had been good. He was seeing her the next day but he hadn't wanted to wait that long to tell her. She felt rather pleased.

'Boyfriend?' Anita asked with a smile.

'Hardly.' Tessa thought a moment. 'I'm not sure what our relationship is—or what it'll turn into. He's very special—but he certainly has problems. For that matter, so do I.'

'What sort of problems does he have?'

Tessa considered. 'He wouldn't want me to talk about him so I won't. It's just that a…previous relationship still affects him.'

'The walking wounded,' said Anita. 'The people who will never trust again. Or, if they do, they get into more trouble. I liked your talk tonight, Tessa. It was useful to me, too.'

'Useful? How?'

Anita frowned and stared into her glass. 'I had a letter from Peter, my ex. He even sent a few pounds and told me to spend them on Sylvia. He wants to get back together with me, says he made a big mistake.'

In counselling you never offered advice. You let your client come to her own decisions. 'So what are you going to do?'

'I'm tempted to have him back. He could be good to me and often I get lonely and I miss a man in my bed.'

'Are those reasons good enough?'

Anita shook her head. 'No. I think he's had another girl, he's lost her and he thinks I'm convenient. I'm

not going to be made use of again, Tessa! I won't
have him back.' After a pause she went on, 'Notice
I'm not asking you for advice, just using you as a
sounding-board.'

'I think that's the best way,' nodded Tessa. 'You
should be independent in as many ways as possible.'

'But you do think I've made the right decision? Do
I stand up and fight?'

'Well, yes, I... Don't do that!'

Anita laughed. 'I knew I'd trick you into agreeing
with me.'

Next afternoon Tessa dressed with care—again. The
weather forecast was good. She wore white strappy
sandals and a sleeveless pink summer dress that went
perfectly with the straw hat she had bought in Reims.
It was only a week since she'd been in France with
James and Lucy, but such a lot seemed to have happened since then. Her life was accelerating and she
found this disturbing.

She wondered where they were going, why she was
both excited and apprehensive. She'd had dates before, been out with other men, and had always felt
that she'd been in control of the situation. But she'd
never been out with a man quite like James
Armstrong.

He was to pick her up at home and she decided to
wait for him outside. She didn't want him coming into
her flat—well, not yet. Very few people were invited
there. It was her own place where she felt most se-
cure.

As previously, he was on time. When the burgundy
sports car drew up beside her and he got out to open
the door for her, her heart actually bumped. She felt

it, it was silly. After all, she'd seen him only two days before—and then they'd had a row.

He was wearing another lightweight suit, in fawn this time, with a darker brown open-necked shirt. And he was beaming.

He saw her into her seat, sat beside her and said, 'The last little worry has disappeared. Remember Lucy being invited back to supper by a lad she met at the concert rehearsal? Well, last night his mother rang me to ask if Lucy could spend the day with them—they're driving to Buxton for the day. I said yes. So now I need to think of nothing but us all day.'

'That's wonderfully selfish,' she said cheerfully.

'That's what I need. That's what we both need. To get away from pain and grief and tension and the A and E department in general. Out of the city into the country. Pretend for a while that we don't have problems.'

She stretched luxuriously in her seat. 'Mmm—sounds like heaven.'

James regarded her silently for a moment, before he said, 'Do you mind if I ask you something?'

Tessa shrugged. 'Not at all.'

'A girl as attractive in as many ways as you are—you're beautiful, outgoing, intelligent, good company—why haven't you been snapped up by some man?'

'Thanks for the compliments,' she said tartly, 'but remember it's a male view to think that the only success for a woman is to land a man. Perhaps I don't want one. Now, where are we going?'

She needed to change the subject.

The car was air-conditioned, which she was very pleased about. Getting into her own little car in this weather was like stepping into a greenhouse. But now they were sweeping across the countryside in cool comfort.

They left town, stayed on the motorway for a quarter of an hour and were now driving across the Cheshire plain. He seemed determined to stick to the minor roads, which was even more pleasant. Tessa loved the greenness, the richness of the fields. It was good to get away.

Eventually they drove into a village called Hartsford. It was pretty, with half-timbered cottages and red-brick larger buildings. The main street was laced with bunting and a large sign proclaimed HARTSFORD VILLAGE SHOW.

'A village show! For a city sophisticate like you?'

'There's nothing like this near London. We're going to enjoy ourselves, wander round, look at exhibits of large vegetables, buy home-made cakes and do lots of nothing.'

'Lots of nothing! Now, that sounds like a great idea.'

So that's what they did do. Before leaving the car, she smeared sun-block over her arms and made James put it on his forehead and the back of his neck. 'You've dealt with people suffering from too much sun.'

'Indeed I have,' he said feelingly. 'In fact, I had one man come in with what he thought was sunburn—asked me if I could prescribe him some cream for these nasty marks on his arms. Nasty marks! It was squamous cell cancer. Reasonably easy to deal with, of course—ultimately he had laser treatment, which got rid of it completely. But it gave him a shock and I'll bet he never sun-bathed again.'

'Don't bet too much,' she told him. 'Some people never learn. James! We're talking shop again.'

'Sorry.' He smiled.

They walked to the field where a collection of marquees housed the show. For half an hour they sat and listened to a brass band. It was very good. Then a local choir sang, and they were good, too. Then there was a fancy dress parade and the best three outfits picked. She didn't agree with the judging but James did, and they argued about it.

There were assorted games to play. There was throwing table-tennis balls into a jar, out of which they promptly bounced. Or they could try to throw hoops round assorted prizes.

'This is terrible,' he whispered to her. 'What do I do if I win that bright blue penguin? It's not even ceramic, it's plastic.'

'If you win you take it home, put it in the middle of the mantelpiece and treasure it. It'll be a family sporting trophy.'

His last hoop went very, very wide.

After all this they felt in need of food, so they went into the tea-tent and had home-made cakes and tea. On the way there they passed the St John's Ambulance tent. She looked at it thoughtfully. 'No,' he said. 'If they need a doctor or a nurse, they'll ask on the PA system. This is a doctor's day off.'

'If a doctor ever has a day off.'

They looked over the secondhand book stall, she bought more home-made cakes and he carried them for her. Then they wandered through the village, looked at the duck pond, the stocks and the old church.

'Are you hungry?' he asked after a while. 'It's nearly half past six.'

Tessa looked at him in genuine amazement. 'It's not! Where has the time gone?'

'Perhaps it passes quickly when you're enjoying yourself.'

'Well, I have enjoyed myself—this has been marvellous. But now you mention it, perhaps I am getting hungry.'

They got back into the car and he drove five miles to a pub by a canal. 'This has been recommended to me,' he said. 'The food is supposed to be very good.'

James booked them a table outside, and since they would have to wait for half an hour they walked along the tow-path. It seemed natural to Tessa to hold his hand. They watched herons skittering by, smiled at the helmsmen as barges slowly chuntered past.

'They're only allowed to go at four miles an hour,' he said, 'or should it be knots? Travelling by barge has always seemed very peaceful to me. A good way to relax.'

'Relax? How long is it since you relaxed, James? I'm surprised you know what the word means.'

He considered. 'I've relaxed today. And I've really enjoyed it.'

'And before today?'

'Well, not for months. But I think it's good to take things easy if you can. I enjoy being with you, Tessa.'

They went back to the pub and had a meal outside. James had a pint of beer and ordered Tessa half a bottle of wine.

'I'll drink it only on condition that soon I can take you out. I'll drive and you can have the half-bottle of wine.'

'All right,' he said. 'That seems fair. So, do you want to go out with me again?'

She thought carefully. 'Very much so,' she said with a smile.

Now dusk was falling. He came round to sit by her side, put his arm round her and kissed her. A long, gentle kiss. If a kiss could be uncomplicated, then this one was. But there was a hint, a promise, of something more to come. 'We'd better stop now,' he said, his voice slightly husky. 'Perhaps we ought to set off back.'

'All right,' she murmured softly.

They talked aimlessly and amiably on the way back. But when they entered the city boundaries his face grew more grim, his answers grew more curt and he hunched his shoulders as if he carried the weight of the world on them.

She teased him. 'You tell me to take things easy, but you don't take your own advice. You look as if you're going back to a whole ocean of troubles.'

He smiled. 'I know. I'm afraid it's my nature. But being with you relaxes me, Tessa.'

'Good.' They were now ten minutes from her flat and she said, 'I know you won't take this for the kind of invitation that it isn't. But it's still quite early. I...don't invite many people back with me but would you like to come in for coffee? We could talk a bit more.'

'I'd like that very much.'

She took him into her living room. It was small compared with the rooms in his house, but for her it was ideal. She wanted somewhere absolutely simple. In her lounge there were two easy chairs, a coffee-table, a wall of books and CDs. There was a small television, a rather expensive stack of radio, tape deck and CD player. And there were candles. She sat him in one of the easy chairs and went round the room lighting candles—on the window-ledge, on the hearth, on the coffee-table. Then she switched off the main light.

'Why so many candles, Tessa?'

It was a hard question to answer, but she tried. 'First, they're beautiful. I've lit candles all my life. It's the soft light they give and the tiny warmth if you get near them. It's a light completely opposite to the hard light you need in medicine. There's something about candlelight that frees my soul, but I don't know what it is.'

A little to her surprise, he seemed to accept her answer. 'I see. So in this soft light can you say things—tell things—that would otherwise be kept hidden?'

'I'll fetch your coffee,' she said quickly.

It was a momentary escape which would soon be over. As she poured from the cafetière she knew that she had to make up her mind. James had been completely honest with her, she knew what it had cost him to tell her his secrets. Why couldn't she do the same for him? She could. She would have to.

But when she returned and handed him his coffee he didn't push her too hard. 'You've never mentioned your family,' he said.

'I'm an orphan.' A flat statement, almost a challenge to him.

'So am I,' he said. 'Just think, we're two little orphans in the storm. It makes me value family life even more though. That's why I get so angry about divorce.'

'I could have guessed.'

'I've listened to all of your recent programmes, I think your advice is very good. Remember a while ago, you were talking to someone called Barry?'

He stared up at the ceiling. In the candlelight his face was a patchwork of planes and shadows. 'I memorised your exact words. You said, "It's a risk you have to take. If you offer something of yourself then you're vulnerable."'

'Yes,' she said carefully. 'But I said a lot more, too. You can't take sentences out of context.'

'That sentence was at the heart of what you said. Why don't you take your own advice?'

'I do! I never say anything that I don't believe in and act by.'

'In the car this afternoon I asked you why you hadn't got a steady man in your life. You said perhaps you didn't need one, and promptly changed the subject. Tell me what you're frightened of. I know there's something.'

She was angry now. 'I suppose Lucy told you! I thought that—'

'Lucy told me nothing!' He leaned forward, looked at her in surprise. 'You told Lucy something that you won't tell me?'

'I thought it necessary at the time,' Tessa muttered. 'I thought it would help. Woman-to-woman sort of stuff.'

'You told my daughter something you wanted to keep quiet about yourself. A secret, in fact. Tessa, I'm a bit…well, I'm a bit overcome that you should do such a thing. Just to help a stranger.'

'It was no great thing. Just an ordinary, trite, sordid story.'

'You can tell me,' he said gently, 'but only if you want to. If not, we'll talk about other things. You could play me one of your CDs.'

'No. I think I'd like to tell you.'

It always hurt to think about this story, it would hurt even more to tell it. But tell it she would. Perhaps one day she would be rid of the pain it still caused her. That day wasn't yet.

'I was in my third year of nurse training. I loved the work. But I loved Colin even more. He was a couple of years older than me, in his last year of medical training. I thought I was truly in love—in fact, I was. It was the real thing. A day wasn't complete unless I saw him and when I did it lit up my life. When I didn't see him I thought about him and I carried his picture with me everywhere in case I forgot what he looked like. I can look back and those days were the happiest of my life. He invited me to live in his flat and we were a couple. I washed for him, I cooked for him.'

She sat there, aware that the tears were rolling down her face.

'So what happened?' His voice was gentle.

'I found I was pregnant. It doesn't matter whose fault it was, these things happen. I was pregnant. So I told him, I told him as soon as I was sure…and he said to get rid of it. I thought he was just shocked, I was shocked myself. But he said get rid of it. When I said no he said I had to choose between it and him. I said it wasn't an it, it was my baby. I wouldn't kill it…or him…or her.

'Well, he certainly wasn't going to support me and an unwanted child, he had a career to think of. And if that was the way I felt, I could get out of the flat.

'So I got out of the flat. I moved into the nurses' home. I didn't tell anybody else I was pregnant, and eight weeks later I...I...I lost the baby. These things happen, you know.'

'Oh, yes,' he said quietly. 'I do know.'

'So I told Colin. I thought perhaps he might... It had been his child and... But all he did was say that it was a relief. I might as well move back into the flat. That was the worst thing of all! It was all he thought of me!'

Silently, James offered her a handkerchief, and she wiped the tears from her face. 'There's no sympathy I can offer now,' he murmured. 'It would be pointless. But I think I know what you went through. So how did it make you feel?'

'For years I wouldn't ever go out with a man I worked with. I had to carry on seeing Colin almost every day and it was too painful. The few men I have seen something of have been from outside hospital.'

'So you have been out with men occasionally?'

'Yes. But I've never really trusted a man since then. I'm wary, I don't want to get too involved.'

'But you're changing,' he said softly. 'You've been out with me and we work together.'

'You're a man. I still suspect you, I can't help it.'

'Tessa, I've been hurt, too. But there's always the possibility of happiness, of something new. For years I didn't believe this, but meeting you has changed my mind. Have you been happy today?'

'Yes,' she said after a while, 'very happy. I don't think I'll ever forget what we've done—though we don't seem to have done very much.'

'I think we've done plenty. You're tired, aren't you? Should I go now?'

'If you don't mind. I've got a lot to think about. My life seems to be changing so quickly. I'm going to have to cope with all these new emotions, aren't I?'

'You'll cope. One last thing, I promised I'd ask. Next Saturday Lucy is in a youth concert in Manchester. I'm going, of course, and she asked if you'd like to come too.'

Tessa nodded. 'Of course I would.'

She stood and he held her for what seemed like hours. He didn't kiss her, just held her to him. His body was rock-like, she could feel the heat of his breath, the steady rise and fall of his chest. There was the scent of aftershave and under it the warmth of his body. Slowly she grew calmer. To her surprise she started to feel sleepy.

Perhaps he could tell this by the heaviness of her own breathing. Finally he kissed her gently on the lips. Then he said, 'I think you should go to bed.'

'All right. I think you're right. Are you going now?'

'I'll sit here by the candles until you shout and tell me you're actually in bed. Then I'll go.'

'All right.'

Her clothes she dropped in a pile, she had the sketchiest of washes. Then she called, 'I'm in bed now.'

His body loomed in the open doorway. 'Goodnight, sweetheart.' There was the click of her front door opening and he was gone. Five minutes later she was asleep.

*   *   *

He rang her next day, in the middle of the morning. She was going to work lates again and didn't have to be in hospital until one o'clock.

'I just wanted to say how much I enjoyed yesterday,' he said, 'and to find out if you were all right.'

'Of course I'm all right! It's just that telling…that story always gets me a bit upset. I'll get over it in time. It's silly of me, I know.'

'Not silly at all. Tessa, we didn't have a chance to talk about it much yesterday, but I would like to see more of you. We're both a bit scared of commitment, but, well, I've never found anyone like you.'

'I've got a friend who says we're the walking wounded,' she said with a wry smile. 'In time the wounded recover.'

'I know that. I'll be in for a while this afternoon. Will I see you there?'

'I hope so.'

She rang off and went and stared out of the window. Another wonderful day. Suddenly she felt extremely happy.

'She didn't want to come in but we persuaded her,' the paramedic said laconically. 'There doesn't seem to be much wrong internally but her face is pretty badly messed up. Police have got the louse who did it.'

Tessa sighed. Every case that came into A and E was a minor tragedy, but domestic violence cases were the worst of all. Sometimes she thought that working there was enough to put you off marriage for life!

She whisked the curtain aside and walked into the cubicle. The figure on the trolley was holding a pad to her cheek. Wan eyes looked up as she entered. 'Tessa!' The word was gasped out.

Tessa stared down, appalled. It was Anita. But Anita with a viciously bruised face, with blood spilling from cuts on her forehead and cheek, a split lip and the dark marks on her neck that showed that she had been partly strangled.

Tessa was a nurse and in a situation like this she could not allow herself to panic, to have personal feelings. She had to do what was best. 'Where's Sylvia?'

Anita's lips moved in what might have been a smile. 'Sylvia...OK. Neighbour's got her... He didn't come near her.'

Tessa didn't ask who the 'he' was. 'Anita, I'll be a minute, just a minute. Hang on till I come back.'

'I'm not going anywhere.'

A distant part of Tessa's mind registered that Anita could joke. Good.

The triage nurse had determined that Anita wasn't too badly hurt, she'd be seen in a few minutes by the junior registrar. But Tessa wanted better than that for her friend. She ran to James's office. He wasn't on duty but she knew he was in. She knocked and opened the door.

'James, there's a friend of mine just been brought in and I want you to see her.'

He looked at her appraisingly and said, 'All right.' He reached for the white coat hanging by the door. 'Tell me what you can before we get there.'

'She was beaten up. A man did it, and she's got a daughter but the daughter's all right. He's her ex-boyfriend and—'

James's voice was gentle. 'Tessa, we're nearly there. I need medical details.'

Of course he did. She provided them. At once.

He nodded. Then he said, 'There's something else, isn't there? Apart from her being your friend?'

She hadn't quite realised it herself, but he was right. 'Perhaps. It's all a bit confusing. I gave her some advice, well, I tried to help her. And now I wonder if what I said caused her to… Well, I feel to blame.'

'I doubt that. But we'll think about it afterwards.' He pulled back the curtain and looked down at Anita. 'I'm Mr Armstrong, Anita. Now, let's see what we can do for you. Just move your hand and I'll look at this cut on the side of your head.'

In fact, there wasn't too much wrong with Anita. Tessa knew that there'd be worse injuries coming in that day. But James stayed longer than was necessary and when he left Anita was much more cheerful. Tessa started to bathe and dress the wounds she had suffered.

'The police are outside,' she said gently. 'They'll want you to make a statement. You don't have to. I can send them away if you like.'

Anita looked obstinate. 'I want to talk to them. There's no reason why he should get away with this. I want him punished. Look at what he did to me!'

'That's the right attitude. But remember, you'll have to go to court. You'll have to face him there, it'll be hard on you.'

'I'll do it. I'm tired of just taking what life hands out. I want to fight back.'

'Good. But just take things easy for a while. Was it that man you lived with—Sylvia's father?'

'Yes, it was Peter. He thought because he'd given me some money he was entitled to move back in, even though I told him I didn't want him. He just turned up in a taxi with his cases. And when I tried to phone the police he started to…he started to hit…' She buried her face in her hands.

'It's over now,' Tessa said, putting an arm round the weeping girl. 'It's over now and you can rest here a while and then we'll see about Sylvia.'

Anita looked up through her tears. 'Sylvia's fine, she's with a good neighbour. Tessa, you were right. I was thinking of having him back but you showed me that would be wrong.'

Tessa tried to hide her dismay. 'I only tried to help you make up your own mind, Anita. Now, try and rest and I'll be back to see you in a while.'

'You've been so good to me, Tessa,' Anita said with a weak smile. 'You showed me that there were people who could care, and that was worth so much.'

'Try to rest,' Tessa murmured.

She had her work to do and James wasn't even officially in the building. But she managed to find a spare ten minutes and asked if she could talk to him.

'I think Anita got hurt because of my advice, James. I told her to stand up for herself, to be independent. I even agreed that she should fight for herself. So she tried—and look where it got her.'

'And now you're feeling guilty. In future will you give different advice?'

'Yes…no…I don't know! Perhaps I'll not advise anyone about anything! We're not supposed to advise anyway, we're supposed to help people to come to terms with their problems in their own way.'

'I'm sure that's what you did.'

Tessa sighed. 'Yes, I did. But Anita certainly knew what I wanted her to do. And I've interfered. I've found her a part-time job at the radio station. She'll not be able to do that for a while.'

They were in his tiny office, legs jammed together under his desk again. He looked at her broodingly. 'Sometimes you have to make hard decisions,' he said, 'decisions that turn out not the way you wanted. You get hurt, I know that. But always making a decision is better than just letting things run on. You helped Anita make a decision and I think ultimately she'll be grateful.'

'Perhaps,' Tessa said. 'But right now she's lying in A and E with her face battered.'

James reached for his wallet, opened it and took out a wad of notes. 'When you went to France with us I said I'd pay you. But you said that taking money embarrassed you. We agreed that I owed you but that we'd talk about it later.'

'This isn't a good time to talk about money,' Tessa said.

'Not for you perhaps, or for me. But money might be important to Anita right now. She can't do the job you got her, she'll have extra expenses. Even a taxi here and there would help her. Give her this, the money I was going to give to you.'

Tessa's first reaction was to say no. But then she realised there was a brutal common sense in what James had said. Right now Anita needed money. It would make her life if not happier, then less miserable. 'Anita would never accept charity,' she said.

'Tell her it's an advance on her salary. To be repaid only when she's fit, well and working.'

'That's a good idea. I'll take the money, James, and thank you so much.' She paused just as she was reaching for it. 'I feel better now. Less guilty, in fact. You knew this would happen, didn't you?'

'It seemed a kind of solution,' he said.

'How would you like to be a guest on my pro- gramme? Give advice?'

He shuddered. 'I've made too many mistakes in my life ever to advise anyone.'

CHAPTER EIGHT

ONCE again Tessa was in James's car, speeding through the early evening with him and Lucy. Having Lucy with them made the trip less exciting but more restful. When she was alone with James, so often she felt that she was on the brink of a discovery, that her life was about to change in some radical way. She needed time. If Lucy was there she had the pleasure of James's company but none of the apprehension.

They were going to the concert in Manchester where Lucy was to perform. Tessa was looking forward to it.

'Have you heard any more about this new job you've been offered?' James asked casually.

Tessa frowned. Recently she had been thinking of other things. 'They implied I'll be offered it,' she said, 'but I don't know...'

'It would mean your leaving the department.'

'No chance,' Lucy shouted from the back seat. 'We need you here.'

'I'll always be a nurse,' Tessa said. 'Even if I took this job, I'd have to work at least part time. But I don't think I could really work at the Halstead.'

'I've always tried to encourage my staff to get on, to take opportunities when they can. And this is a good chance for you. But I'd miss you an awful lot. The department needs you.'

Lucy didn't hear the message but Tessa did. James would miss her. The department was less important.

The concert was given by six gifted young people. James told her that there was an internationally renowned music school in Manchester, five of the soloists came from it. Lucy was the sixth.

She was the first player after the interval. Tessa watched her walk across the stage, obviously slightly nervous. She was wearing a full-length dress, which Tessa had helped her choose, and she looked lovely.

There was a quick introduction and then she started to play. The moment she did so, her nervousness disappeared. This is what Lucy did, and she did it well. Tessa wasn't an expert, but she thought the playing was fantastic.

She looked at James's face as he watched his daughter. So often his expression was cool, or forbidding, or even angry. Tessa knew that this was only half of his character, that he had a loving, giving side that few people knew. And that side was showing now. He loved and was proud of his daughter. She meant so much to him. Tessa felt warmed by the love even though she wasn't part of it.

Lucy finished playing, to quite exceptional applause. She stood, bowed to the audience. Then she looked at James, and Tessa saw a quick, secret smile. Lucy knew how she was loved, and loved James in return.

There were many people to consult, forms to be filled in and decisions to be made—but eventually it was agreed that Lucy could come and shadow Tessa in the A and E department.

'Arrange it while I'm away from the department if you can,' James had said. 'She sees enough of me at home. I want her to see what the work is really like. It's good of you to do this for her, Tessa.'

'She's not going to just watch,' Tessa said, 'I'm going to work her. I'll show her what nurses have to do.'

Of course, there were incidents, scenes when it wouldn't be proper for Lucy to be involved, but Tessa intended to give her a fair taste of the good and the bad bits of a nurse's work.

Lucy was good. She sat six-year-old Martin on her knee and amused him while Jack peered then probed in his ear to get out the button Martin had pushed in. She fetched cups of tea, chatted to distressed patients who were waiting to see a doctor. And Tessa told her a little about having the right instruments ready for the doctor on the tray, about maintaining a sterile environment.

She was sitting on a stool, watching as Tessa carefully cleaned a deep gash in a roofer's arm. Then Jack leaned over to suture it. Tessa glanced up, saw the paleness of Lucy's face, the fact that she was rocking slightly on her stool.

'All right for a minute?' she asked Jack, and nodded towards the silent figure.

Jack looked up, and realised the situation at once. 'Of course. I can finish up here, no trouble.'

Tessa led the unobjecting Lucy away, found her a trolley to lie on. 'Was it the sight of all that blood?' she asked. 'Don't let it worry you, I fainted the first time I went into Theatre.'

'No. I just felt a bit… Don't tell Dad, will you?'

Tessa looked at her more carefully. 'Have you been having any kind of problems? Period pains or anything like that? Something you can't tell your father about?'

'No. And Dad and me, we're all right about things like that. I'm sorry to be a pain when you've gone to so much trouble to help me.' She tried to struggle upright. 'I'm OK now. Let's get back.'

Tessa eased her back on the trolley. 'You look terrible,' she said frankly. 'You're going to rest and you don't move from there till I tell you to. So close your eyes and I'll be back to see you in ten minutes.'

Tessa left to go back to Jack but after taking two paces she turned and said, 'Is this something new? The first time it's happened?'

'Three or four times over the past couple of weeks,' Lucy said, and smiled weakly. 'Nothing much. We growing girls suffer from things like this, don't we? I didn't want to worry Dad so I kept it from him. And I don't want you to worry either.'

But Lucy didn't improve much through the morning. And after three hours Tessa said to Jack, 'I want you to look at Lucy. Forget whose daughter she is, forget that she's supposed to be shadowing me. Pretend that she's been brought in by an ambulance after collapsing in the street.'

Jack looked at her thoughtfully. 'All right,' he said. 'But she's only fourteen. We need a parent's permission.'

'James is about to go into a meeting,' Tessa said. 'But I'll probably be able to catch him first. I'll phone him.'

She remembered what Lucy had said, and tried not to worry James too much. 'Lucy fainted,' she said briefly. 'I'd like Jack to look at her—is that all right?

We need your permission. And the message from Lucy is, don't fuss.'

James laughed. 'I know she's in good hands,' he said. 'Let me know if it's anything serious.'

Obviously, he thought that it wasn't. Tessa wondered.

She fetched Jack.

'Just come and look at her,' she said. 'I'll help her undress and take a history.'

Surprisingly, Lucy didn't object to being asked to undress. As she did so Tessa casually asked her how long she had been feeling ill and were there any other symptoms.

'It only started about two weeks ago,' Lucy said, 'I just felt generally rotten for a while, then it went. But it's been getting worse over the past couple of days.'

'And you didn't tell your dad?'

'He's got enough to worry about. Please, don't tell him now. I thought this was just a cold or something. Though I haven't been sneezing or coughing.'

'It'll probably pass soon,' Tessa said. 'Like you said, one of these teenage girl things.' But she felt slightly worried, it seemed more serious than that.

Jack put his head in the cubicle, motioned for her to come outside. Tessa told him the little she had learned. 'Have you told her father?' he asked.

'I have. He's in the hospital, some kind of very important financial meeting. Shall we wait a while and get in touch if it's necessary? I know Lucy's desperate not to trouble him.'

'I don't like it,' Jack said. 'I always like a family member to be present if it's a child we're looking at. But I guess she's among friends here.'

He entered the cubicle and smiled at Lucy. 'Now you can see what it's like from the other side of the bed,' he said, 'and I want you to mark me for kindness and bedside manner.'

'You haven't told my dad?' Lucy's voice was anxious.

'Not yet. But we may have to soon. Now, let's look in your eyes.' Jack quickly checked her pupils and went through the routine examination—pulse, blood pressure, respiration rate, temperature. Lucy's pulse was fast, her BP and temperature both a little too high. He looked at her chest, frowned when he saw the large bruise there. 'Did you bump into something, Lucy?'

'Not that I can remember. It's just a bruise, it doesn't hurt.'

'No nosebleeds, no bleeding from the gums?'

'Nothing like that.'

Have you noticed a swelling in your abdomen at all?'

'Not really.' There was a tiny spark of spirit left. 'And I'm not pregnant. There's absolutely no chance of that, I can guarantee.'

'Well, we'll cross that off the list of possibilities.'

Tessa watched as Jack pulled down each of Lucy's lower eyelids, looked quickly inside. 'You lie there a bit longer, Lucy. Tessa's going to take some blood from you. We'll send it for analysis and then we'll know a bit more.'

Tessa reached for the sterile-packed kit.

'Well, what's wrong with me?'

'I'm not sure yet. But we'll get there in time. Just lie here and rest and I'll be in to see you later.'

Tessa followed him out of the cubicle. 'Well?' she asked. 'What do you think it is?'

Jack looked uncomfortable. 'I really don't know,' he said. 'I know she's a friend of yours and that makes things difficult. It's hard treating people you know, I don't want to speculate. Make sure I get those blood results the minute they come in.'

'Why did you look in her eyes?'

'The insides were pale, far too pale. Have you noticed if she's been looking paler recently?'

'Yes,' Tessa said after a minute's thought. 'Perhaps she has.' She didn't say what she thought, what she knew Jack suspected. Sudden paleness, a possible very low blood count. It could be lots of things. It could be leukaemia.

The results didn't take too long. It wasn't Tessa's place to look but she did anyway, scanning the sheet, looking at the various results. Lucy's white-cell count, red-cell count and platelet count were all abnormally, ridiculously low. Tessa felt sick.

She took the results to Jack. 'You'd better get her father down here,' he said. 'I'll ring the haematology ward. We'll try and jump a stage, get the consultant down here instead of a house officer or junior reg.'

'Harry Jowett is a friend of James,' Tessa said. 'He'll be here at once.'

She rang the office of the hospital CEO at once.

'Is it really important?' the receptionist asked coolly. 'Are you sure it can't wait? Mr Armstrong won't like being called out of the meeting, and I know he's got some very important suggestions to present to the committee. Why not wait half an hour?'

Tessa tried to control her rage. 'It is important and

it can't wait. Please get Mr Armstrong to the phone now. Tell him this is Nurse Tessa Calvert and it's about his daughter.'

'Oh. Has she been in an accident?'

'Not exactly, but it's very, very important that I speak to him at once.'

There was silence for a minute. 'Oh, very well. Please hold.'

James's voice was full of concern. 'Tessa? Is Lucy OK?'

Tessa took a breath. 'Jack's had a look at her and we think that she might be...she might be ill.'

His voice was deathly calm. 'I'll be there at once, of course. Will you thank Jack for his concern, Tessa? And thank you, too. Tell Lucy I'll be right with her.' He rang off and Tessa sighed with relief.

When she got back to Lucy's cubicle Jack was outside, talking to Harry Jowett, the haematologist. Harry looked up from the sheet of blood results in his hand and smiled at her briefly. 'James is coming?'

'He'll be right here,' Tessa said. 'Do you think—'

Harry held up his hand. 'I don't think anything yet, only that this young lady needs an instant transfusion. We need the results of more tests before we even begin to think. Now, would you like to go and sit with Lucy for a while? I'm sure she needs a friend.'

'All right. She is my friend so I want to be here when you talk to James!'

Harry raised his eyebrows at this, but merely said, 'If James wants you here, that's fine.'

'In that case I'll—'

'Harry? I didn't expect to see you here.' James turned the corner of the corridor. He smiled at no one, though his voice was calm. He looked intimidating, though Harry didn't appear to notice his forbidding appearance. He said, 'I was very properly called out, James. I'm about to admit your daughter to my ward and I shall need your signature and so on.'

'Admit Lucy! Why?'

'For tests. There's something we need to determine.' He handed over the blood results. 'Look at that.'

Tessa watched James as he glanced at the sheet. She saw the shock hit him like a blow, he even rocked slightly. He paled, and she knew he was fighting for control. 'These are too low, Harry! Why didn't I notice? She must have—'

'James! What she must have is more tests. We'll start on them at once. This time I'm the doctor, you're the parent. I don't want you worrying, trying to diagnose. We just don't know yet! Now, she'll get the very best attention this hospital can offer.'

'I know that, Harry,' James said, 'but don't tell me not to worry. If she was your daughter, would you worry?'

'Of course. Now, you go and see Lucy and then I suggest you go back to your meeting. If I can borrow Tessa here for a minute, she can go with Lucy to my ward and get her settled. That OK, Dr Harris?'

'Of course,' said Jack.

'And I'll phone you the minute I have any results at all,' Harry said to James.

'Thank you.' It was like an iron shutter coming down. Tessa saw the hardness coming over him. Whatever James felt, he wouldn't let it show. His feelings were the business of no one but himself. She wanted to reach out, to tell him that it was all right to show emotions other than anger, but she guessed that it wouldn't be a good idea.

She followed him into the cubicle, saw him bend to kiss his daughter, then she moved out again. He needed to have time alone with Lucy. But he was out within a couple of minutes, and when he spoke his voice was normal. He might have been looking at one of the many casualties that were brought in off the street.

Harry had left now and it was up to her and Jack to get Lucy up to the haematology ward. James said conversationally, 'I think Lucy was very lucky, this happened when she was working with you two. A good professional job. Well done. Now, I think I have a meeting to attend. I'll see Lucy later.'

Tessa and Jack watched his back as he walked rapidly down the corridor. She wasn't surprised by his seemingly emotionless response. James was being tortured. But by not leaning on anyone, by not letting anyone else share in his pain, he was making that pain doubly hard.

Tessa took Lucy up to the ward, saw her settled but left as the nurse assembled a giving set. Lucy was to have a transfusion at once. 'You will phone me if there's anything at all that I can do?' she asked the sister.

'Of course. Don't worry, we'll look after her.' And Tessa had to be content with that.

She went back to A and E. 'Got an RTA in four,' Jack said laconically. 'Go and take a history, see what you can do, will you, Tessa? I've got an eye injury in one, I'll be with you in a minute.'

'On my way.' Life in the department went on.

*   *   *

Eventually it was time for Tessa's shift to end. There had been no news from the haematology ward but she didn't ring as she knew there was no news. After handover she walked to the ward, told the sister she was there and sat in the waiting room. She was alone there. The doctors were with Lucy.

After an hour James walked into the waiting room. He was still in his suit and looked completely unruffled. But his face had changed. It looked as if it had been carved out of stone, as if he had never felt anything in his life.

'It's good of you to wait, Tessa,' he said. 'Very thoughtful.'

'What's wrong with Lucy?' She knew her voice was trembling but she just had to know.

'It's too early to tell with complete certainty. Harry thought she could have leukaemia. I guess so did I. But he's done a blood film test and there were no abnormalities. So he took a bone-marrow sample. The few blood-producing cells she has are normal. So it's not leukaemia. It seems as if Lucy has contracted aplastic anaemia.' His voice was quiet, courteous, as if he were discussing the weather.

Mostly Tessa dealt with trauma, she wasn't an expert on this kind of thing. She tried to remember what she knew. It wasn't a cancer, that was the good news. How serious was aplastic anaemia?

'Just how bad is that?'

His voice was still remote. 'It couldn't be worse. Harry's classified it as very severe. About eighty per cent of people die of it within a year. Lucy could be dead in a few weeks.'

Tessa stared at him, unable to comprehend the

words he had just spoken so quietly. 'What? Dead? In a few weeks? But there must be… Surely they—'

'I'm certain that Harry Jowett will see that she gets the very best of attention.'

'Is that all you can say? James, this is your daughter's life we're talking about. Can't you show any emotion at all? Have you no feelings?'

'Yes, I have feelings. But you must let me deal with them in the way that suits me best. And this is the best way.'

'I very much doubt that!'

For the first time she saw a small smile. 'I should have known that you would have a view on the subject. Now, would you like to come and see Lucy? She's very sleepy but I'm sure she'd be pleased if you were there.'

Lucy looked much younger than her years as she lay in bed. Her eyes flickered a moment and she said, 'Hi, Tessa, I'm causing trouble again.' Then she went back to sleep.

'Aren't you going to hold her hand?' Tessa managed to gasp to James.

He shook his head. 'She's asleep now. We'll only be in the way here for a while. We may as well go.' He brushed the hair from his daughter's forehead and bent over to kiss her there.

Just for a moment Tessa thought she could see the pain in his eyes. But it was instantly gone.

It would be far more convenient for the ward if they left now, and James had arranged to return later. The staff nurse came over and said to him, 'We have the number of your mobile. If there's any reason at all, we'll call you.'

'Thank you.' He turned for one last look at Lucy and walked out of the ward, Tessa following behind.

She blinked when they got in the corridor. The sun was shining. It was only early evening. Around them were people going about their affairs, happy with life, unaware of the shock she and James had had. 'Come and walk with me in the grounds for a while,' she said.

'All right.' He seemed indifferent to what he was to do.

She led him out of the nearest door and they set off across the grassy lawns that extended between the buildings. It was warm, there were little groups of people sitting about, chattering, drinking from plastic cups. None of them knew what she and James were feeling. She led him behind the hospital where there were fewer people, where there were still a few of the great trees that had been there for years. They sat on a bench in the shade of an old oak.

'I have to thank you for your professional skill,' he said. 'I gather it was you that first noticed that something was seriously wrong with Lucy.'

'Don't be so controlled! It's good to let go, to feel, to let other people know that you are feeling. It's no disgrace, she's your daughter. Why can't you let go? It doesn't hurt you to show your emotions, you know.'

'It does hurt to feel. I know that. Lucy has been the centre of my life. Without her I don't know what I will have to live for. Not even my work will mean anything. Tessa, I just can't lose her!'

For the first time, a crack in his armour. For a moment Tessa felt guilty that she had pushed him into making this declaration. But she knew that ultimately owning up to the pain would make it easier.

'Perhaps you won't lose her. Don't prejudge what might not happen. You have to live a day at a time, enjoy each day for what hope it brings you.'

'I know you're right. But it's something I've had to say to people in the past. It's easy to say—now I know how little comfort it brings.'

'What are you doing this evening when you've seen Lucy? It'll do you no good just to sit with her all night. You've got to be fit to work.'

The question seemed to puzzle him. 'Do this evening? I'll go home, I suppose. Though it'll be lonely without her.'

He could admit to being lonely. Well, that was a start. But the next step was hard for her. She had difficulty speaking. 'Would you…would you like to come back to my flat? You might want some company.' She went on, 'You could stay the night if you liked. There's a…there's a spare bedroom if you want it.'

He turned to look at her. 'I thought I was blessed with Lucy. But with you I'm doubly blessed. Now you go home and I'll go to sit with Lucy.' He leaned forward, kissed her softly on the lips. 'If anyone could comfort me now, it would only be you.'

She watched as he walked across the grass and disappeared into the nearest building. Then she walked to her car. She had invited him to stay, she had to prepare.

There was a supermarket on the way home. She wasn't going to spend the whole evening cooking— though it might have been therapeutic. Instead, she would buy the best of ready meals.

Probably he would be hungry. She knew that one of the effects of grief was that people didn't realise they had gone without food. And when they were presented with a meal, they were ravenous. So she bought a couple of bottles of wine, fresh soup, a beef casserole and some expensive ice cream. When her trolley was loaded she walked to the checkout. Then she stopped and walked back to the medicine section.

James phoned her at half past nine that night. 'There's been no change in Lucy's condition, she's sleeping peacefully. Do I still have an invitation to stay with you?'

'You have. I've got enough food here for three, you'll have to come.'

He laughed. She was glad he could. 'I'll call in at home for my toothbrush. Should I bring some wine?'

'There's no need. I've bought a couple of bottles myself. In about half an hour?'

'I'm looking forward to it.' Then his voice softened. 'Do you know how much I'm looking forward to it, Tessa?'

'Half an hour,' she said briskly.

She was still in the jeans and T-shirt she had put on when she'd changed from her uniform. She thought for a moment, then went and swiftly showered and put on a floral summer dress. Then she brushed her hair and added a touch of make-up. Looking good made her feel good. It might make him feel better, too.

He arrived in exactly half an hour. When the bell rang she felt a moment of apprehension. She had invited him almost without thinking. Perhaps it hadn't been such a good idea. But he was in trouble and she wanted to help him. She went to let him in.

He had changed, too, into a light shirt and chinos. He was carrying an overnight bag. When he put it down, she put her arms round him. His body was firm, she could feel the muscles through the thin material. She laid her head against him and thought that she could stay here for ever. Something told her that he would be happy to do that, too. For a moment or two, all problems seemed distant. But she knew they'd come back.

Reluctantly letting go of him, she said, 'There's a meal ready. I've waited for you and I'll bet you're as hungry as I am.'

'Lead me to it,' he said.

She had thought about candles—he had liked them last time but perhaps this wasn't the occasion to have a full candlelit meal. So she compromised by lighting just one or two. He looked at them.

'Candles,' he said. 'Like you, I spend most of my life under the harsh light of the department. Candlelight is softer, it makes me think that life isn't hard and clear-cut. And I need that right now.'

'You don't often tell me what you need,' she murmured. 'Let me light some more.' So she did, and switched off the main light. The flickering flames transformed his face, and she couldn't tell what he was thinking.

As she'd guessed, he was ravenous. It didn't surprise her to notice that he enjoyed the wine but drank only a moderate amount. James wouldn't let himself lose control.

He didn't say much, except to compliment her on

the meal. 'Not exactly my finest hour as a cook,' she said cheerfully. 'Everything was ready-made.'

'The meal was good. The company made it wonderful.'

'That's two compliments you've paid me in less than ten minutes. James Armstrong, you're slipping.'

'I ration myself. Or I ration you. The rarer a thing is, the more it is wanted.'

'I shall look forward to my ration. One a week, is it? One a fortnight?'

'Much more than that. Anyway, how often do you compliment me?'

'That's different. Men don't need reassurance.'

It was an amiable, slightly pointless conversation, but she thought it was what he needed. He had to relax—if it was possible—for a while to think of other things besides his daughter.

When the meal was over she fetched a pot of coffee and they sat together on her couch. Then she said, slightly abruptly, 'You're going to phone the hospital, I know. Why don't you do that and then have a bath? My phone's in the hall.'

'I do want to phone. But I'll use my mobile so I can sit next to you as I do so. Whatever I hear I want you to share.'

She squeezed his arm but said nothing.

There was no news from the hospital. The ward sister said that Lucy was sleeping peacefully and she would ring if there was any change. 'Just what I expected,' James said, his voice hollow. 'Why did I ring?'

'Because you feel powerless and you had to try to do something.'

James shook his head. 'Why do you know everything I think before I think it?'

'Not everything, James.' She reached over and took
his hands in hers. First she looked at his face, still
unreadable in the candlelight, then she bowed her
head.

The words were harder to say than anything she
had said in her life. 'While you have a bath I can
make you up a bed in the spare room. Or, if you want,
I have a double bed…' She tailed off, uncertain what
to say next, but knowing what she wanted, what she
hoped James wanted too.

James leaned forward, but then drew back. 'Tessa,
do you mean this?' His voice was hoarse.

'Yes, I do.'

He kissed her quickly, and was gone.

She blew out most of the candles but carried just
two to her bedroom and stood them on her dressing-
table. Then she undressed, slipped on a long nightie
and got into bed. She was facing her dressing-table
and the two candles were reflected into six by the
triple mirror. Ghost-like behind the lights, she could
see her own face.

James came into the room. He was wearing a dark
dressing-gown. She could not make out his expression. 'Tessa, I don't think you know how much I want
to get in there with you but are you really…?'

She spread out her arms to him. 'Stop talking and
come to bed.'

So he did. They lay side by side, his arm under her
head, and for a while were content just to hold each
other. It was a warm night, all that covered them was
a sheet. Tessa could feel its softness against her naked
shoulders. She knew that, however tired she was, she

wouldn't sleep just yet. From her open window came the sound of traffic, the distant thumping of a ship sailing up the estuary. On James's breath she could smell toothpaste and there was the scent of an expensive soap on him. Not hers, she thought. He must have brought it with him.

And she was in bed with him. Perhaps all he wanted was comfort, the closeness of another person. Well, that was fine by her. Today must have been so hard for him. There was only so much emotion a person could take before exhaustion set in.

He kissed her. A gentle, almost tentative kiss, his lips soft on hers. For a while she was content just to enjoy it, but then she wriggled closer to him. Her breasts pressed against him, she pushed her leg between his.

Now the kiss was more passionate and she grasped the back of his neck, held him to her. This was what she wanted. It came almost as a shock to her to realise just how much she needed him. His lips left hers, trailed down her body. He eased her onto her back and she sighed then called aloud as his mouth claimed her breasts. This was so good!

But they were both still dressed. 'I want to feel you, James,' she mumbled. 'I want to feel all of you.' She pulled herself away from him, threw off the sheet and crossed her arms to drag off her nightie while he shrugged off his dressing-gown.

Now they were sitting on the bed, both naked, facing each other. His hands grasped her shoulders, stroked the length of her arms, then moved across her breasts to her waist. 'You're so beautiful,' he murmured. 'Tessa, so beautiful.'

She thought he was also beautiful. The candlelight

seemed to burnish his skin, make his body seem exotic, mysterious. She reached out for him and then stopped.

'You're a doctor and I'm a nurse,' she said. 'We're intelligent people. This is wonderful but...'

She could see the dismay in his eyes and she was so happy she had to giggle. 'I don't mean that, silly,' she said. 'I mean we're going to be sensible. Look in the top drawer of my dressing-table.'

He did, and found the packet she had placed there. 'I bought them in the supermarket earlier,' she told him. 'Just in case they were needed.'

'Tessa! I—'

'Be quick and come back to bed.' She lay there, felt the night breeze caress her. Then he came and lay by her side again.

As he kneeled over her and entered her, she knew it was an act of longing, of desperation. He had suffered so much today and she was the one he had chosen to help him in his anguish. But now his passion grasped her too, and as their bodies shook together in the final climactic moment she knew it had meant as much to her as to him.

And that was so much! They clung to each other, shuddering, amazed at the depth of feeling.

After a while Tessa went to open the window even further, and then lay by his side. The cool air whispered across their heated bodies. They held hands.

'You gave me so much, Tessa,' he whispered. 'Now I just don't know what to think, what to feel, all my emotions are in turmoil. There's Lucy and there's you. I just can't cope with it all.'

'Sweetheart, you don't have to cope. Just be.

You're here with me and if that makes you as happy as I am, then it's plenty.'

'Yes,' he said softly, 'you've made me happy.' He lifted her hand to his lips, kissed it. 'Tessa, I've not said this to any woman in years, but I think...' His voice faltered. 'That is, I'm very fond of you.'

'Fond, James Armstrong, fond? You're only fond of me? What kind of a passionate declaration is that? You're a brave man. Come on, I dare you to say it! Tell me what you really think.'

'And you're a hard woman, Tessa Calvert. All right, I'll say it. I think I love you.'

'There, that didn't hurt too much, did it? And I think I love you, too, James. But for the moment, no plans, no announcements, no changes, the same life as before. You've got Lucy to think about, and I want to help you. When she's better, when you're not worried sick about her, then we'll think again.'

'When she's better?'

'She will be,' Tessa said confidently.

CHAPTER NINE

'I KNOW it's easy for me to sit here and advise people what to do. One girl I know listened to me, did what I suggested. And she got hurt. Not mentally or emotionally, which is bad enough, but physically. She got beaten up. For a while I thought of giving up this programme if that was the kind of result I got. But the girl was kind to me, she said the stand she had taken was right. So today's message is be safe, but try to do what is right for you.'

It was Saturday morning, and Tessa was driving to Manchester with Ray again. 'Last night's programme was quite something,' he said. 'We've had an awful lot of phone calls about it. You've started something, Tessa.'

'The only phone call that counted was the one from Anita. I asked her if she minded if I talked about her. She said no. It made her feel as if she had come out on top. So I guess I'm pleased, too.'

'Good. Now, we're going to see this group again, apparently for a chat. But I've heard that they're going to offer you a contract. How do you feel about it, Tessa?'

There was an urgency in Ray's voice. Tessa knew he very much wanted her to sign the contract, but she still wasn't sure. 'I'll have to have time, Ray,' she said. 'My personal life is a bit confused at the moment.'

'Confused? Want to talk about it?'

'No, Ray. Let's wait and see what happens at the meeting. I might not be offered anything.'

But she was. They were swept through the outer office, offered the excellent coffee again and beamed at by Les, Andy and Cath, the same trio who had interviewed her.

'We were pretty close to a decision,' Cath said, 'and then we listened to your programme last night. That decided us. The writing, the delivery were brilliant. We think you could have a great future in radio, Tessa, and we'd like to offer you a contract. Are you going to join us?'

This was it, the moment of truth. 'I'm very keen,' Tessa said honestly, 'but this would be a big change for me. I need time to think.'

Obviously this wasn't the answer the three had expected, but they covered their surprise well. 'Why don't you talk to Ray about it?' Cath said after a while. 'We'd want you to work with him anyhow. Just don't take too long. We need to think about next year's schedules. But we can fit you into a training programme at a week's notice.'

'I'll be as quick as I can,' Tessa promised.

'You'd be so good at this job,' Ray said as they drove home, 'and if you did well, I'd do well. But you're a friend, Tessa. Do what's the best for you and that's fine by me.'

'You're a friend too,' she said, and leaned over to kiss him on the cheek.

Tessa visited Lucy at least twice a day, but not at the same time as James. She was getting very fond of the girl, but she thought Lucy wasn't looking any better.

Every day her face looked a little more wan, a little thinner. But Lucy still had her father's determination. She was a fighter.

'How are you getting on with Dad?' she asked one day.

'Fine, just fine,' Tessa said airily. 'I see him around the department quite a lot.'

'I'm sure you do. How many times have the two of you been out together? Or, for that matter, stayed in together? You know, socially.'

Tessa tried not to show how warm she was feeling. 'We see something of each other, yes. Why, has he said anything to you?'

Lucy laughed. 'Of course he hasn't. He wouldn't, you know that. But when I casually mention you he perks quite up a bit.'

'We're getting to be good friends. And we're both worried about you.'

'Well, thanks. Have you done it yet?'

'Done what?' Tessa asked.

'Done *it*. You know, what men and women do together in bed. Had sex. Have you and Dad been to bed yet?'

'Lucy! The very idea! You can't, you mustn't...' Tessa felt a red tide of embarrassment in her face.

'That's all right. You don't have to tell me, I can guess from the way you're looking. That means he won't be able to tell me off again.' Lucy paused, she was feeling weak. 'Not that you need my approval, but you and Dad are OK by me. You make him happy. And you're the nearest to a mother that I've ever had.'

Suddenly Lucy had changed from someone sharp-witted and street-wise into a forlorn little girl.

'Having you as a daughter would be a challenge,' Tessa said, 'but I think I'd like it.'

For the moment Harry was treating Lucy with a drug called cyclosporin. One possible long-term treatment would be the use of immunosuppresive drugs. But this was far from ideal, there were many possible unpleasant side-effects. The best thing would be a bone-marrow transplant.

'There has to be a match between donor and recipient,' James told Tessa, 'otherwise the transfused marrow is rejected. Usually a sibling is best—but Lucy hasn't got any brothers or sisters. I had my marrow tested, of course, but sadly it's not a match.'

'So what can you do?'

James shrugged. 'It's just possible that there might be a compatible donor who has nothing to do with Lucy. Harry is searching the database, he might just find a match. It's funny, lots of people are willing to give blood but bone marrow is something else.'

'Can anyone get on this database?'

'Of course. Harry Jowett will arrange it. You give a sample of marrow, it's analysed and the results fed into the computer. The chances are that you'll never be asked to have your marrow harvested. But the procedure isn't too unpleasant and you'd have saved someone's life.'

'I like the idea of saving the life of a complete stranger,' Tessa said thoughtfully. 'I'll phone the department tomorrow.'

It didn't take long and it didn't hurt. Tessa lay on her back and the nurse erected a little screen just under her chin so she couldn't see what was happening.

There was a local anaesthetic and then the vague feeling of pressure on her chest. The marrow sample was being taken from her sternum, a thick bone very close to the skin.

'That's fine,' the young house officer said after a few minutes. 'We've got our sample and you can go and sit down with a cup of tea for half an hour.'

Tessa sat upright. 'Could I see it, please?' she asked. 'Look, I'm an A and E nurse, I'm used to blood—even my own.'

The doctor grinned and held up a glass tube. Inside was a bright red substance, but somehow it was different from blood. 'This is it. But in a little while it'll be nothing but an entry on a computer. You know there's a good chance you'll never be asked to be a donor?'

'I know. But it feels good just to make the offer.' She swung her legs over the side of the bed and the nurse helped her upright. It hadn't taken long.

'Do you get many people coming in to offer to give samples?'

'No. We'd like thousands more. The more there are on the database, the better the chance of getting a match.'

'How would you like to make an appeal on local radio? I could arrange it,' Tessa offered.

James stayed at home every second night and on alternate nights he stayed with Tessa. Sometimes they talked, often he came in very late and did nothing but sit by her on the couch, his arms around her.

They had made a pact when they made love in her bed. They'd said they loved each other, but the word was never mentioned again. They wouldn't think about themselves nor talk about their future until Lucy was well again.

Tessa knew what James was doing and could sympathise. When he was not with her or sitting with Lucy, he was trying to lose himself in work. His face grew thinner, at times his eyes showed the pain he was feeling, but in the department he was super-efficient.

'That man frightens me,' Jack said to her one day. 'I can guess what he's going through but he never shows it. I've never seen such control, Tessa. Do you think it's good for him?'

'No. But I've tried talking to him, it's the way he is. When I say he's stressed he just laughs. And he doesn't smoke, drink or take any pills. He just works.'

'Well, the department is getting the benefit. Now he's here it's running like clockwork. Are you OK with him?'

It was now known and generally accepted that James and Tessa had some kind of relationship, but no one questioned her.

'We're getting on fine, but at the moment all he can think about is Lucy.'

'I can imagine that. He makes me think of a volcano—quiet and peaceful and pleasant. But I wouldn't want to be near when it erupts.'

It was that night that James finally talked about Lucy. He had been with her all evening after talking to Harry Jowett. Tessa knew the minute he came in the door that something was wrong. She kissed him as she always did, and he kissed her back. But she could tell he wasn't with her, his mind was far away.

'Tessa,' he said, 'I don't know what...' Then his voice trailed away.

'Eat and drink first,' she said. 'Your blood sugar must be at rock bottom. Then, if you want, we can talk.'

So he had the meal she had prepared and she knew that he had no idea what he was eating. Then they sat side by side and she waited for him to begin.

'Lucy's getting weaker,' he said slowly. 'Harry's not saying very much, just that he'll try an aggressive course of immunosuppressive drugs. But he doesn't really want to. I keep on wondering if there are things he's not telling me.'

'You've been in this position yourself! He won't tell you because he genuinely doesn't know. He may suspect, but he just doesn't know!'

'True.' He gave her the bleakest of smiles. 'This is going to make me a different doctor, Tessa. I thought I knew what my patients were going through—or at least what their relations were going through. Certainly I *knew* it—but now I can *feel* it as well.'

'I always knew you were a big softie underneath,' she said tenderly, 'but you certainly hid it very well. Now, let me take you to bed.'

Tessa was like James now. It was better when there was work for her to do, things to keep her mind off Lucy. But this particular night things were slack. She was working through till eleven and the evening seemed to stretch on without end. James was in the department, he'd told her he now hated to go home. He was lost there without Lucy and spent most of his free time either with Tessa or in the department. He had just gone up to see his daughter. Tessa would go later. They both had to go. But it was a painful experience.

Tessa was sitting in the little department rest-room, holding a cup of coffee that had gone cold, when Sally looked round the door.

'There's a lady here wants to see you,' she said. 'She wanted to see Mr Armstrong and when I found that he wasn't in she said she would see you.'

'Patients wait in the waiting room,' Tessa said. 'We don't do appointments.'

'I don't think she's a patient. I do think you should see her, Tessa.'

Tessa put down her cup and ran her fingers through her hair. Later on she'd take it down, comb and put it up again. No need to let all her standards go. She walked down the corridor towards the figure Sally had pointed out.

The woman was gorgeous—and it was obvious that she knew it. She was dressed in the height of fashion—a greenish silk dress that must have cost hundreds, an expensively simple haircut, shoes of the finest, palest leather. Her face was immaculately made up, her figure slim. Tessa was dressed in scrubs and felt frumpish. And she didn't like the amused scrutiny she was under.

The woman spoke. There was perhaps the slightest trace of a foreign accent. 'Tessa Calvert? I need to speak to Mr Armstrong urgently. Could you tell me where he is, please?'

Tessa didn't like the way the woman spoke to her. 'Mr Armstrong isn't on duty but he's very busy. If you'd like to leave me your name I'll give it to him when I see him.'

The woman smiled icily. 'I would like to speak to him at once. And I know he would like to speak to me.'

'I'm afraid I can only offer to pass on your name.' Tessa wasn't going to be browbeaten.

'Very well. I will give you my name.' The woman paused, a look of malevolent triumph on her face. 'My name is Michelle Trenet. I am Mr Armstrong's wife.'

'Ex-wife actually,' James said tiredly, 'though Michelle never did bother much about trifles like that. Married or not married, it was all one to her.'

It was later that night and James had come round to visit Tessa in her flat. He was supposed to stay the night with her, but had told her that he would have to stay at home.

When Michelle had announced who she was, Tessa had phoned the haematology ward at once and had got through to James. He'd heard the news of his visitor in silence. 'Can you send her up here, Tessa?'

'Of course. James…I was going to visit Lucy later. Should I not come?'

'Lucy loves seeing you, you know that. But…it might be an idea if you missed tonight.'

'All right.' Tessa had been disappointed.

Now James had arrived but just, he said, for a short while. He didn't want any of the meal she'd prepared as he'd taken Michelle out to dinner.

'It was Lucy's last chance,' he said. 'I had to write to Michelle, I had to try everything possible. But I'm surprised she's come so quickly, and I'm surprised that she's willing to offer her marrow. Michelle never liked pain and especially pain for other people.'

'So where is she now?'

'She's staying with me. She'll have the test in a couple of days, she says there are things she has to sort out first. She says she wants to get to know her daughter.'

'How do you feel about that?'

He shrugged. 'I can only think about Lucy. If Michelle can help her get better…and she is the girl's mother. Perhaps at long last some kind of maternal feeling has surfaced.'

'Perhaps,' Tessa said in a strangled voice. She had to step carefully here. But didn't James know what he was doing to her? Then she felt ashamed. He saw a hope of his daughter's life and was delighted, and she should be delighted with him. 'You didn't tell me how attractive Michelle was,' she said. 'I can see why you married her.'

'I'm not sure you do. I'm not sure myself.'

Well, that was vaguely encouraging. 'Will you be staying at home all the time from now on? Not coming here to stay with me?'

He looked uneasy. 'I think that would be better while Michelle is there. She's an awkward, demanding woman, Tessa. I daren't do anything that might send her off in a temper. I've got to see if her bone marrow is compatible.'

Some mother, who might rush off in a temper, Tessa thought, but wisely said nothing. 'In the department Michelle asked for me by name,' she said. 'How did she know me?'

'I mentioned you in my letter. Said you'd been very good to Lucy. Perhaps it wasn't a good idea.'

'Probably not. She doesn't like me.'

James made no attempt to contradict this statement, she noticed. He looked even more embarrassed than before and went on, 'Tessa, much as I want to—and

I really do want to—I just couldn't make love to you and then go home to my ex-wife.'

'No,' she said dully. 'You couldn't. That's very proper of you, James.'

He glanced at his watch. 'I suppose I should be going. See you in the department tomorrow?'

'I'm on days tomorrow. Yes, I'll see you then.' She stood so he could kiss her, and for a moment everything was all right. 'Remember what we said in bed, James,' she whispered. 'I love you.'

'And I love you, too, sweetheart.' But his mind was obviously somewhere else and he left quickly after that.

Tessa went to her kitchen, looked at the meal she'd prepared. She'd gone to a lot of trouble. But now she wasn't hungry and for a moment she was tempted to take it and throw it all in the bin. But that would be foolish. She reached for the foil. It could all be frozen.

If there was a chance that Michelle could help Lucy recover, that was fantastic news. At this time it was right that James should think of his daughter. But didn't he realise that she, Tessa, had feelings, too?

She remembered what James had said about believing that marriage should last for ever, about not giving up easily on it. Did he still believe that? Tessa had a distant feeling of dread.

Tessa had been visiting Lucy for quite some days and she wasn't going to give up now. But when she walked down the ward she was glad to see she was the only visitor.

'What do you think of my flowers?' Lucy asked. 'They're a bit much, aren't they? There's more outside, you know.'

'Perhaps they are a bit…excessive,' Tessa said cautiously, surveying the bunches of orchids and gladioli. 'Who brought them for you?'

'Michelle. She had them sent this morning. I don't think the sister was very pleased.'

'I can understand that. Too many flowers makes work for the nurses. You call your mum Michelle?'

'Well, I'm not going to start calling her Mother or Mum or Ma. And she's French. Perhaps it should be Maman. It's just a bit late for that, don't you think? Fourteen years too late.'

'Possibly. Er, what's it like, having someone… someone new in the family?'

Lucy shrugged. 'OK, I guess. She's got plans for me, says when I'm better I'm to go and stay with her in this big house in France. We can make music together. She's a violinist, you know. I think I'd quite like that. There's a lot of stuff written for violin and piano.'

'She seems to have everything planned,' Tessa said, wondering what other plans Michelle might have.

'She does.' Lucy turned her head on the pillow to squint up at Tessa. 'How's Dad taking having Michelle back?'

'I don't know,' said Tessa, being absolutely honest. 'We haven't talked much since she arrived. And you know how he hides his feelings.'

'Don't I just.'

'The thing to remember,' Tessa said, 'is that he loves you and he's worried about you and that's all he can think about at the moment.'

'I know.' Lucy's eyes were closing. 'I think I'll

sleep a bit now. You'll come and see me again, Tessa?'

'I'll come and see you soon,' Tessa promised.

Work was at its hardest when Michelle came to see her that afternoon. Tessa was hot, there was blood on her apron and someone had been sick down the side of her uniform. She thought she probably smelt a little and she didn't feel at her best.

Michelle, of course, was immaculately turned out, this time in a dark blue dress that echoed her eyes. Tessa tried to hide her irritation.

'Mr Armstrong should be in his room,' she said curtly.

'I'm afraid not, he told me he has arrangements to make. But I didn't come to see him, I came to see you. You finish at five do you not? James said so.'

'If everything is calm here then, yes, I do finish at five.' She didn't like James talking to this woman about her.

'Then perhaps we can have a talk, go for a little drive. I would like to get away from this place and its smells and its atmosphere.'

'It's where I work,' Tessa said coolly. 'I like it. What do we have to talk about?'

'We have to talk about Lucy and about James. I know he thinks a lot of you, he has said so. But we will not speak here. Outside at five?'

'I may be a little delayed,' Tessa muttered. 'Now, if you will excuse me, I have work to do.'

It would have pleased her if there had been a reason for staying on after five, but for once things were quite easy so she showered, did what she could with her hair and changed into her going-home outfit—a pair of jeans and a light blouse. She was aware that she looked dowdy by the side of the sophisticated Michelle.

What did Michelle want with her? Tessa felt that she was being outmanoeuvred, she was unsure of what was about to happen. She wished James was there.

Michelle waiting for her outside the department, inconsiderately parked on the double yellow lines. Her car was something silver and continental, and Tessa thought it looked expensive.

There was a speed limit in the hospital grounds but Michelle ignored it. There was a queue of cars waiting patiently to drive onto the main road but Michelle jumped the queue and roared onwards, accompanied by the blasting of horns and more than a few curses.

'You drive very fast,' Tessa said. 'There was an old woman there, trying to get across the road.' What she wanted to say was that Michelle was the worst-mannered driver she'd ever seen, but this wasn't the time to start an argument.

'Life is too short to hang about. I go for what I need and I needed to get onto the road. The others can queue if they wish, but not me.'

She drove, quite expertly Tessa had to admit, towards the outskirts of town, then she turned into a quiet road that bordered a park and pulled up in the shade.

'You are wondering what we have to talk about,' Michelle said. 'First, I wish to thank you for what you have done for Lucy—and for what you have done for James.'

She reached into her handbag, took out a packet of thin cheroots and lit one. Tessa didn't like the smell, but it was Michelle's car so she supposed she couldn't object.

'I know you have a regard for Lucy. We both want the best for her. She's a pretty girl, isn't she? And you can tell at once that she is my daughter.'

Michelle turned to face Tessa. Yes, there was a resemblance in the colouring and the large eyes. But Lucy also had her father's generous mouth and determined chin. 'Yes, you do look alike,' Tessa muttered.

'Good. I am glad that you can see it. And certainly she has my musical talent. This must be nurtured, it must grow. Tessa, my daughter needs a family, she needs a mother. I am sure I can count on your help to bring this about.'

'You've waited fourteen years to discover that your daughter needs a family?'

Michelle shrugged. 'James and I, we parted. I am sure he has told you his version of the events. I am sure that you will realise that there is always more than one side to a story.'

'Perhaps,' said Tessa. She knew she was being manipulated but she didn't know what she could do about it. 'I will do all that I can to help James and Lucy. But they have their own minds to make up.'

Michelle gave a little tinkling laugh. 'Of course. Now, I came here because James begged me to. He wants me to have a test to see if my bone marrow will help Lucy, and if it will then I shall donate some. In the future she might need more. It would be better if I were with them, don't you think? If I were abroad it would all be hard. It would be best if Lucy had me with her as her mother.'

'You are her mother.'

'But at the moment divorced from her father. I think it would be best if I married James again. You know, he always says that marriage should last for ever, don't you?'

'Yes,' faltered Tessa. She couldn't believe what she was hearing. Was Michelle really saying this? She tried to fight back. 'Do you mean that James has to marry you or there'll be no marrow for his daughter? For your daughter?'

Michelle laughed again. 'Of course not! I shall do what I can. But I spend many months away from home. It would be better for Lucy if I were closer. Perhaps if I had more time with James, perhaps if only the two of us were left to sort out our problems, then things might be better.'

Tessa realised that it wasn't James who was being blackmailed, it was herself. She left James to Michelle or Michelle would go. And there would be no transplant.

Michelle was watching her closely, knew that she had an advantage. 'I know that you and James have been very close. He's an inventive lover, isn't he? I've missed that. But now we're together again it's all coming back. Last night was so good!'

'Last night! He slept with you last night?'

Michelle looked at her in surprise. 'But of course. Why not? He still thinks we are married. It was exciting after so long. You know, the same but different. I know he's slept with you, he's told me and I don't mind at all. That's the way men are, isn't it? But he is still my husband.'

'No, he isn't, you're divorced! He's free to marry who he likes! I'll tell him about this little conversation and see what he says!'

'As you wish. But if James is free to marry who he likes, then I am certainly free to do what I like. Perhaps we should keep this conversation to ourselves.'

Michelle threw the cheroot out of the window. 'And now I must take you back. I have an appointment with—is it Harry Jowett? There is the matter of a marrow donation to discuss.'

There was nothing more Tessa could say.

CHAPTER TEN

TESSA left a message on James's office answering machine saying that perhaps it would be better if he didn't come to see her that night. He had Lucy to think of and Michelle, and it wasn't a good idea for him to be distracted. He didn't ring her back, but next day he came to find her in the department. As ever, she was busy, but he took her to one side.

'I'm sorry I didn't see you last night, sweetheart. But there were arrangements to be made and I have to keep an eye on Michelle. She's a bit demanding but...she's Lucy's best chance.'

Tessa looked at his careworn face and felt a great surge of love for him. This wasn't the time to express it, though. She reached up to kiss him on the cheek. 'Don't worry. Lucy comes first, she must. And I quite understand: Perhaps we could—'

From a cubicle further down the corridor, Jack's head appeared. He nodded at James and then said, 'I could do with a hand, Tessa. Like now.' Tessa hurried off to help.

A patient had struggled and pulled out a catheter. Tessa helped Jack calm the man and reinsert it, and then waited for the sedative they'd given to take effect. When she came out of the cubicle James had gone.

She knew what she had to do. She would tell James what Michelle had told her, how she had threatened them—and Lucy. Then Tessa thought again. She knew James so well now, recognised the uncompromising streak in him that would make him do what he thought was right, whatever the consequences. If she told James about Michelle's threat, Michelle would be told to go. And with her would go Lucy's chance of life. Tessa swallowed. It was a chance she dared not take.

At lunchtime she went up to see Lucy. Lucy was getting weaker every day, but there was still a spark in her eye, and she had the same sense of humour, though her voice was quieter now.

'Michelle wants us to go on tour together,' she whispered. 'Violin and piano, mother and daughter. But I want a life of my own first. I'd rather be a soloist. Then perhaps piano and violin, daughter and mother. But I'd still appreciate the marrow.'

'You performers are all the same,' Tessa said, her smile hiding just how upset she was at seeing Lucy's weak state. 'You have to have top billing.'

'You bet. You get nowhere accepting being second.'

Very true, Tessa thought, but she said nothing.

She stood to move her chair nearer Lucy's head and a voice behind her said, 'Just going, Tessa? Then I shall have your chair. We must be careful not to overtire poor Lucy. Not too many visitors.'

There was Michelle, as radiant as ever. For a moment Tessa thought of arguing. But what would be the point? Michelle had the whip hand. Tessa squeezed Lucy's hand and left.

It was no good feeling sorry for herself. Tessa left another message on James's answering machine saying she would be out all evening and he was to get some sleep if he could. Then she went round to see

Anita, who had discharged herself from hospital as soon as she could to get back to Sylvia. Tessa had had a phone call from her saying that she was well, and would Tessa call when it was convenient?

Another glorious evening, and Tessa drove round to Anita's flat. Anita answered her knock. The bruises on her face had faded but Tessa could see where the stitches had been. But Anita was happy. She gave Tessa a beaming smile, stepped forward to hug her. 'Tessa! So good to see you. Come inside, there's someone I want you to meet.'

Tessa managed a strained smile. Who did Anita want her to meet? Please, please, not the man who had put her in hospital. Stranger things had happened, Tessa knew.

A woman was sitting in the living room, an older woman whose face looked as if she might be stern. She was wearing a pinafore and her iron-grey hair was in a bun. But she wasn't stern at the moment. She was bouncing little Sylvia on her knee, making the child shriek with pleasure. 'Pat-a-cake, pat-a-cake baker's man. Bake me a cake as fast as you can…'

'This is my Aunt Sylvia,' Anita said, managing to be both shy and proud at the same time. 'Aunt Sylvia, this is Tessa Calvert, the lady who has been so good to me.'

Aunt Sylvia transferred baby Sylvia to her left knee and offered Tessa a hand. 'I'm very pleased to meet you, Miss Calvert. In general I don't think much of people who offer advice in the papers and on the radio. But you're different. You make refreshing sense.'

Bewildered, Tessa looked from Anita to the two Sylvias. 'But I thought you were… I gathered that you…'

'We had a row,' Aunt Sylvia announced with some satisfaction, 'a blazing row. Things were said on both sides that were perhaps foolish. But that's all over now, I hope. I think we've both learned.'

'We're going back to the Isle of Wight,' Anita said, 'where baby Sylvia can have a proper family. I'm sorry to give up the job you found for me, Tessa, but I'll be glad to get home.'

'You're all going to live together again?'

'No. Not a good idea. Anita can have a little house not too far away and I hope to see a lot of her and my new niece, but I think we need separate lives.'

'Perhaps that's a good idea,' Tessa said faintly.

'This is all down to you, Tessa,' Anita said. 'Remember when we had a drink, and you said that a lot of trouble was caused by people not talking? Well, that night I wrote to Aunt Sylvia.'

'I was very glad she did,' Aunt Sylvia put in. 'I'd been worried. I...thought perhaps I'd been wrong.' This was obviously something that didn't happen very often. 'But now we've got things sorted out. Perhaps I'll be better at being an aunt the second time round. That letter gave us both a second chance.'

'We've just been talking about us,' Anita said. 'That's selfish. How are things with you, Tessa?'

'Fine,' Tessa said, 'just fine. Couldn't be better.'

Apparently she could sort out other people's lives. Why couldn't she do something with her own?

'Sometimes choices are difficult. Sometimes whatever you do someone is going to be hurt. But remember that you are a person too. Your hurt matters. It's not always selfish to think of yourself.

Fine sentiments, Tessa thought after she had written them out, they'll make a good programme. Pity I can't apply them to myself.

She had stayed up till the small hours of the morning, thinking, wondering, planning. She had tried something she had recommended on her programme, writing out the problem to see if that made a solution any more obvious. It didn't.

If she didn't leave James, Michelle wouldn't give Lucy the bone marrow if hers proves compatible. If she told James how she was being blackmailed, James would demand an explanation from Michelle—and Lucy still wouldn't get the bone marrow. Tessa couldn't take a chance with Lucy's life. It would be best if she just disappeared from the scene.

She had a fortnight's holiday time owing. She checked with Human Resources and, yes, she could take it at once. Then she said she would be resigning. This caused no end of trouble. She was an excellent member of staff, the department really needed her. Wouldn't she, please, reconsider? No. She was going for personal reasons.

She phoned Cath, Les and Andy in Manchester and they were delighted that she could start a training programme on the following Monday. They would book her into a hotel at once.

It was better to keep moving, keep working. She went home and packed, and then she wrote a letter to James.

It was hard. Working on the radio had made her used to expressing her thoughts clearly, but writing this letter was hard. Exactly what did she want to say? She tore up half a dozen versions before she was satisfied. Not that 'satisfied' was the word.

I have enjoyed myself so much with you. But now it is obvious that our lives are following different directions and so it's better that we part cleanly. I shan't come back to Halstead Hospital, I have a new career. Give my love to Lucy, I know she'll get better. Kind regards, Tessa.

Kind regards! Was that all she could offer him?

She couldn't just leave, she had to keep some contact with the department. For a start she wanted to know how Lucy was so she told Jack where she was going and gave him her telephone number at the hotel in Manchester.

Jack was devastated. 'You can't go! You hold this department together! We just can't manage without you.'

'There are other nurses, Jack.'

'No, Tessa, you're an essential part of what's done here, you know that. And what about James? Have you had a row with him?'

'We don't talk about James, that's flat. And, Jack, under no circumstance do you give him my telephone number. Have you got that?'

He held up the notebook he carried with him everywhere. 'It's in here. And no one looks in here but me. I won't tell him. Tessa, are you sure we can't—'

'No,' she said, 'we can't.'

Tessa was shocked to discover how easy it was to close down her life. It was done in an afternoon. She phoned Ray who was delighted to hear that she was going to Manchester. There would be no problem in cancelling her talks, he had a local history programme that could take its place. An agency would let her flat and store her possessions—all she had to do was phone them and send a key. She wrote brief notes to her many friends. And then she drove to Manchester, the tears flowing in rivers down her cheeks.

Work with the new company was hard. She signed a contract; for the first six months it could be terminated on either side at two days' notice. They wanted complete commitment. She sat in on the rehearsals of other programmes, learned how much more complex broadcasting was when it went out to a national audience rather than just half a city. She wrote out scripts, discussed them with Cath, rewrote them, recorded them and listened to work out her mistakes.

Her hotel room was pleasant, with an area where she could eat and work. She never went out. Her meals were sent up to her, often she left them half-eaten. She tried to lose herself in work. But just writing wasn't as much fun as before. She needed the excitement of life on a ward to really come alive.

Tessa didn't think about James. She had made her decision. He was out of her life and she wouldn't, couldn't, think of him. But sometimes, when she got into bed, it was hard.

Ten days passed. She was sitting at her desk, rewriting a script about coping with the menopause. 'Try to make it a bit more light-hearted,' Cath had urged. 'It's good but it needs to be just a bit more positive.'

Tessa wasn't feeling light-hearted and positive. But she was a professional, she would do what she was asked.

There was a knock at the door—presumably a waiter had come to collect her largely ignored dinner trolley. 'It's open,' she shouted absently. 'Come and get it.'

She heard the door open behind her, then click shut. Strange, she thought vaguely, usually there's the clink of cutlery and then he pushes the trolley through the open door. An unusually silent waiter or... She glanced over her shoulder.

'Good evening, Tessa,' James said.

She had hoped that the worst of her suffering was over. But when she saw him, a great surge of emotion broke over her. This was the man who should have been hers. How could he torture her like this? Why didn't he leave her alone?

He was dressed casually and in one hand he held a bottle, in the other two wineglasses. What was happening?

She looked at his face and for a moment was taken back to that moment she'd first met him, all those weeks ago, at the Black Lion. The compressed lips, the hunched shoulders. James was tired. He was also blazingly angry. 'We're going to talk,' he said.

Well, she could be angry, too. How dared he come to disturb her like this? 'I don't want to talk,' she said stiffly. 'I've got nothing to say to you.'

'That's not like you. I thought you always had something to say. Wasn't that your main point? If people can talk they can usually sort things out? A pity you don't listen to yourself sometimes.'

In one corner of her room there was a coffee-table and two easy chairs. He sat in one of the chairs and started to uncork the bottle of wine. 'Sit down.' He gestured at the other chair. 'We'll have a drink together.'

'What happens if I don't want a drink with you?'

'Too bad. You'll just have to suffer. Now, *sit down*!'

So she did. He poured two glasses, passed one across to her. 'This is a dry Saumur, the wine I gave you when you first came to see Lucy.'

She accepted the glass. 'I remember it, it's a lovely wine. What is this, a romantic reunion?' She hadn't wanted to say it—it had just come out.

'Some romantic you are! No, it's just to remind you of how things were when we first met. When there was so much in front of us, though perhaps neither of us realised it.' His voice was softer now.

She could cope when he was angry. But when he was gentle with her it was so much harder. 'How did you find me?'

'I knew you wouldn't be able to leave without leaving a contact number so someone could tell you about Lucy. I guessed it would be Jack Harris but knew that nothing would persuade him to tell me. So I waited till he was in the shower and then looked in that notebook of his. Your number was in the back.'

'That was underhand and dishonest!'

'I'm ashamed of myself,' he said, sounding anything but. Then his tone changed. 'Incidentally, do you know how much you've hurt Lucy?'

In fact, she thought she did. But it stabbed her like a knife to hear him say so. There was nothing she could say and she sat there, silent.

'I explained a few things,' he said after a while. 'I think she understood. Now.' His voice grew angry again. 'I think you're a hypocrite. There's a theme running through every one of the programmes you made. That is, that you can always try to talk. If there's a problem then both sides should try to talk about it. Right?'

'I suppose so,' she muttered.

'Then why don't you practise what you preach?'

There was nothing she could say. Nothing would make her tell him about Michelle's threat.

He smiled at her. 'Before you say any more, let me tell you a few things. Michelle has left, we won't see her again. She will not marry me, she will not have Lucy as an accompanist. She has gone for good.'

Tessa was horrified. 'But what about the bone-marrow transplant!'

'I told you, you have to talk. We knew that my bone marrow wasn't a good fit. Neither was Michelle's. But the database found a practically perfect match—a young doctor somewhere in Devon. The marrow was harvested, flown up and inserted.'

Talking about his daughter made James's face look even more haggard and Tessa's heart went out to him for the worry he must be feeling. 'She's not out of the woods yet, but at least we can see a path. Harry says she'll recover—it'll take time but she'll recover.'

Lucy would recover! Tessa rose and ran round the table to hug him. 'She's going to recover! James, that's so, so good. Oh, James, I'm so happy!' She could feel the tears on her cheeks. She seemed to have spent rather a lot of time crying recently.

Gently, he eased her away. 'I did say Lucy is missing you. And now she feels a bit guilty because she knows what her mother did to you.'

Lucy knew? Tessa couldn't believe that. 'What does she know about what her mother did?'

James looked slightly uncomfortable. 'She worked it out, Tessa. She worked it out and I didn't. She started by being certain that you wouldn't just leave without saying goodbye to her. So why had you gone? What threat could have made you disappear? Michelle was the only new thing that had come into our lives. What might she have done? Lucy worked it out, and when she asked me if I thought Michelle might have emotionally blackmailed you into disappearing, I thought about it and it suddenly made sense.'

'So you told Lucy?'

'I didn't need to. She guessed from the anger in my face. I would have liked to have kept it from her, it's a nasty thing for a daughter to know about her mother. But Lucy has no illusions where Michelle is concerned.'

'James, that's terrible!'

'I know. But Lucy seems to be coping with it well enough. I don't think she ever really liked Michelle. You will come back and see her soon?'

'Of course I will! Tomorrow.' Then Tessa sat in appalled silence. How could she have been so wrong—about everything? 'So where does that leave us?'

'Well, we're talking. I suppose that's a start. Do you know what it's been like without you, Tessa? Worrying about Lucy and without you by my side to help? I thought I'd found someone at last that I could spend my life with. And then you just went. Tried to cut me out of your life, just like that.'

'Cutting you out is right, James. You've no idea how it hurt. But I didn't think... I'd been betrayed before, and when you slept with Michelle I—'

'I did what?' Tessa quailed at the sheer volume of his voice. 'Slept with Michelle! Whatever gave you

that lunatic idea? I would no more sleep with
Michelle than… She told you that, didn't she?'

'Well, it seemed…possible.' But the more she
thought about it, the less possible it seemed.

'Possible! Some time before that I said I loved you.
Did you think that that was just possible?'

She had to try to fight back. 'Actually, you said
you thought you loved me, and I had to drag that out
of you.'

'You also said you loved me. And I believed you.
What are we arguing about, Tessa?'

'I don't know,' she said. 'Why don't you come
over here and kiss me?'

After a while she whispered, 'So, whatever happens, we talk. We can sort things out.'

'We can sort things out,' he agreed. 'There's your
resignation, this new job, seeing Lucy—but we can
sort things out.'

Tessa was sitting on his knee, her arms round his
neck, her head on his shoulder. It was so good to be
there but he might be getting uncomfortable. 'How
did you get here? she asked.

James seemed surprised at the question. 'I drove,
of course.'

'And we're going to finish that bottle of wine.
You'll be over the limit. Would you…would you like
to stay the night?'

'I thought you'd never ask,' he murmured softly.

Tessa wanted to leave at once. But she had signed a
contract and so she stayed for a further two days training before she could leave. Cath pleaded with her to
stay, but Tessa's mind was made up. She went back
to be with James. The next night she stayed at James's

house. He said he had a surprise for her, and led her into his conservatory. It was dark now and she looked around her in wonderment. He had bought every type of candle imaginable—long, short, thin, fat, white, coloured. And he had set them everywhere so they reflected off the glass and made the plants seem dark, mysterious shadows.

'James, this is magic!'

He bent over to kiss her. 'You said it was magic the first morning in France.'

'It was magic then, too. And it's not going to change, is it?'

'No. Never.' He ran his fingers down from her temples to her chin. His voice was hoarse. 'Sweetheart, you know I could look at your face for ever. And I will.' She was content to stand there, just looking at him, but after a moment he led her to the couch. 'Sit here with me and in a moment I'll fetch us some wine. You were some time talking to Lucy—what did you talk about?'

Tessa and James had been to see Lucy together but, inevitably, James had been called away.

'Well, you told her the news that we're going to get married.'

'So I did. And she was delighted. She was so happy she cried, Tessa.'

'So did I,' Tessa pointed out, 'and usually I don't cry. But I was happy, too.' She wrapped her arms round his neck, lifted her legs across his lap. 'Anyway, James, for us girls the announcement is only the beginning. There's all sorts of arrangements to be made. I'm only going to have one bridesmaid, and that's Lucy. But she's insisting she picks the dress.'

'Sounds like my daughter.'

Tessa leaned forward to kiss his cheek. 'Only your daughter for a while, James. Soon she'll be *our* daughter.'

'Our daughter.' He smiled into his wife-to-be's up-turned face. 'Our family.'

Modern Romance™
...seduction and
passion guaranteed

Tender Romance™
...love affairs that
last a lifetime

Sensual Romance™
...sassy, sexy and
seductive

Blaze
...sultry days and
steamy nights

Medical Romance™
...medical drama on
the pulse

Historical Romance™
...rich, vivid and
passionate

27 new titles every month.

*With all kinds of Romance for
every kind of mood...*

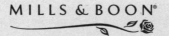

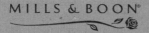

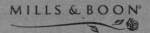

2 FREE

books and a surprise gift!

We would like to take this opportunity to thank you for reading this Mills & Boon® book by offering you the chance to take TWO more specially selected titles from the Medical Romance™ series absolutely FREE! We're also making this offer to introduce you to the benefits of the Reader Service™—

- ★ FREE home delivery
- ★ FREE gifts and competitions
- ★ FREE monthly Newsletter
- ★ Exclusive Reader Service discount
- ★ Books available before they're in the shops

Accepting these FREE books and gift places you under no obligation to buy, you may cancel at any time, even after receiving your free shipment. Simply complete your details below and return the entire page to the address below. *You don't even need a stamp!*

YES! Please send me 2 free Medical Romance books and a surprise gift. I understand that unless you hear from me, I will receive 4 superb new titles every month for just £2.55 each, postage and packing free. I am under no obligation to purchase any books and may cancel my subscription at any time. The free books and gift will be mine to keep in any case.

M2ZEA

Ms/Mrs/Miss/Mr ....Initials...................................
                                                            BLOCK CAPITALS PLEASE
Surname ....
Address ....

....

....Postcode.....................

Send this whole page to:
UK: FREEPOST CN81, Croydon, CR9 3WZ
EIRE: PO Box 4546, Kilcock, County Kildare (stamp required)